U0010299

小王子

Le Petit Prince

安東尼・聖修伯里——著　　綠亞——譯

晨星出版

愛藏本 084

小王子【中英雙語版】

Le Petit Prince

作　　者｜安東尼・聖修伯里（Antoine de Saint-Exupery）
中文譯者｜綠亞
英文譯者｜ Ray Chen

責任編輯｜郭玟君
校　　對｜郭綾茵、劉思敏
英文插畫｜安東尼・聖修伯里（Antoine de Saint-Exupery）
中文插畫｜曾銘祥
封面設計｜言忍巾貞工作室
美術編輯｜張蘊方

創 辦 人｜陳銘民
發 行 所｜晨星出版有限公司
台中市 407 工業區 30 路 1 號
TEL：04-23595820　FAX：04-23550581
E-mail: service@morningstar.com.tw
行政院新聞局局版台業字第 2500 號
法律顧問｜陳思成律師

讀者服務專線｜ TEL：02-23672044 / 04-23595819#212
FAX：02-23635741 / 04-23595493
E-mail：service@morningstar.com.tw
網路書店｜ http : //www.morningstar.com.tw
郵政劃撥｜ 15060393（知己圖書股份有限公司）
印　　刷｜上好印刷股份有限公司

出版日期｜ 2015 年 10 月 15 日
十 三 刷｜ 2024 年 2 月 6 日
定　　價｜新台幣 199 元
ISBN 978-986-443-052-9
Printed in Taiwan

國家圖書館出版品預行編目資料
小王子 / 安東尼・聖修伯里（Antoine de Saint-Exupery）著；綠亞譯
臺中市：晨星，2015.10
愛藏本；84
譯自：Le petit prince
ISBN 978-986-443-052-9（平裝）
CIP 876.57　104016548

所有的大人都曾是孩子

吳淡如

小王子是一本童話，也可以不是一本童話；是一個寓言，也可以不是一個寓言。但如果你不是圖書館的圖書分類人員，不必因此傷腦筋。

它是什麼都不重要，如果你要爲它的屬性爭辯得面紅耳赤的話，你就落入了聖修伯里的「寓言」之中，變成那個誓言只關心重要事情的「商人」，所謂「重要事情」在小王子的字典裡是有點諷刺性的，比如：

假如你跟大人們說：「我看到一棟玫瑰色磚塊砌成的漂亮房子，窗戶上綴滿了天竺葵，鴿子們都棲息在屋頂上。」他們絕對對那棟房子沒有任何想法。你必須說：「我看見一棟價值十億的房子。」他們就會大叫：「那一定是一棟很漂亮的房子！」

我想聖修伯里一直是個孩子，在他心裡，在法國人眼裡，在全世界看小王子的人

的靈魂裡，他就是那個小王子，不肯長大，永遠不會長大。他在四十四歲那年的七月三十一日早晨，駕著飛機離開科西嘉島，從此不見蹤影，五十年來所有小王子的讀者，無不在悲傷之餘發揮想像力，認爲他跟小王子一樣，你永遠找不到他的屍體，他會回到他的星星上，在夜晚，你仰頭看星空，會看到五億小鈴鐺，他就在其中的一顆星上，因爲有他，所有的星星都變得有意義……

所以幾年前，證實在科西嘉島附近海域找到他失事的飛機殘骸，沒有人認爲這是「好消息」。他會每天把花兒放在玻璃罩下，並小心翼翼守護著他的小綿羊，不是嗎？

小王子在全世界擁有可怕的讀者群，不過聖修伯里一定希望我們不要太關心，否則我又會變成只對數目有興趣的、第四個星球上面的商人。

讓我們來關心眞實的故事本身。

小王子是一個很好看的故事，很動人的故事，很適合孩子看的故事（不管是現實的孩子或心靈的孩子），也很適合大多數已經變成有點無趣大人的人。

當你看一本書的時候，你可以變成一個再創造者，這就是一本好書了。如果不分

你的教育程度、職業、年齡、性別和國藉、人種都可以會心微笑，用自己的方法去讀它，那更是一本動人的超級好書了。小王子是這樣的一本書。

這樣的讚美，我並不覺得肉麻，它確實爲我打開一面非常壯觀的窗戶。第一次看小王子時，我十二歲，正處於懷疑自己在世界上完全不被了解的年齡，我的國中一年級國文老師送我小王子，讓我發現了生命的一個出口。故事啊，多麼美妙的天籟，在我心中，做一個說故事的人，變成一種神聖的職業。我也不再懷疑，爲什麼「大人」們不了解我呢，爲什麼大人們了解事情的方式，和觀看世界的角度，和我完全不一樣呢？我依然質疑，但我可以想像自己在地球旅行，不時和小王子交換一個知己的微笑。那時的小王子，對我來說是一個志同道合的朋友。

後來我變成了一個「大人」——長大了的人，我忽然發現自己又從小王子中讀到了新的東西。看哪，我旁邊的世界，充滿其他「大人」（再也不心懷天眞，不可愛的人）的世界，竟然像小王子所造訪過的小行星上的人一樣！

有穿著貂皮，孤獨坐在自己星球上的國王，只想「理性」的下命令控制一切；有些人（其實我們都是）像「驕傲自大的人」，只愛被崇拜，除了讚美什麼也聽不見；有些人像酒鬼，自暴自棄只爲想忘記自己的自暴自棄；有些人像「商人」，只爲數字忙個半死，想佔有再佔有，其實對他們的佔有物非常無助；有些人遵守「規則」如同點燈夫，不知自己爲誰而忙，爲何而忙；有些人是寫大部頭書的地理學家，只關心死的東西，對有生命的一切一點也不感興趣。這時候，小王子是我憤世嫉俗的朋友。

後來，我又在小王子中讀到了生命的矛盾律。

國王說，我相信我的星球有一隻愛叫的老老鼠，我偶爾判它死刑，那麼它的生殺大權就操在你手裡，但每一回你都得饒它，因爲它是我們僅有的犯人。

——驕傲自大的人說，崇拜的意思，就是你認爲我是這個星球上最帥、穿得最漂亮、最有錢、而且最聰明的人；雖然，星球上只有他一個人……

——「爲什麼喝酒？」小王子追問。「爲了遺忘！」酒鬼說。「遺忘什麼？」「爲了遺忘我很可恥。」「爲什麼可恥？」「因爲我喝酒！」

大人總是矛盾的。小王子也是矛盾的。他愛他的玫瑰花卻又不知怎麼愛她，他離開她但又想念她；玫瑰花也是矛盾的，她愛他、依靠他，卻折磨他；狐狸是矛盾的，它要小王子馴養它，但又在他離開時捨不得他……

愛總是矛盾的，聖修伯里的矛盾是所有人的矛盾。

這時，小王子是一個有同情心的天使。

後來，當我的弟弟離開這個世界，無助時我會翻開小王子，讀到「你知道……太遠了。我不能帶這個身體走，太重了……」，我也把自己交給悲傷，每一個像鈴鐺般的星星，也都化成了淚水。我只能祈禱著，小王子在其他的星球，有更可愛的旅程……像聖修伯里所堅信的，離開是一個旅程的新開始，是一種出發，是另一個飛翔的開始。

所以，如果，如果你有一天到沙漠旅行，請不要匆匆趕路，如果有個頭髮是金黃色的小人兒出現，他愛笑，又不肯回答問題，你就知道他是誰了。萬一有這種事，請安慰安慰我吧。捎個口信告訴我，他回來了。

你知道嗎？我不想做個「大人」，因爲我一直不肯在心裡忘記，小王子。

小王子這樣的結束，我的嚕嗦，也這樣的結束罷。

希望所有讀到這本書的小孩都能原諒我，首先將這本書獻給一位大人。

我有相當充足的理由：這個大人是我在這世界上最要好的朋友。

還有另一個理由：這位大人瞭解每件事，即使是有關小孩的書也一樣。

以及第三個理由：這個大人住在法國，他既飢餓寒冷之際需要一些鼓勵。

如果我所說的這些理由都還不夠好的話，請不要介意我把這本書獻給曾經是小孩的他。

所有的大人都曾經是小孩，雖然，只有少數的人記得這件事。

因此，我將我的獻詞更改：

獻給　里昂・維德——當還是小男孩的他

聖修伯里　寫於美國

我六歲的時候，在一本書上看到一張很有趣的插畫，那本書叫做《大自然的眞實故事》，內容是描述關於原始雨林的故事。那張插圖畫的是一隻蟒蛇正在吞食獵物的模樣。你看，就是上面這張圖。

書上寫：「蟒蛇連嚼都不嚼，把獵物整個吞下去以後，就一動也不動，直到牠們長眠六個月，消化完所有吃下的食物。」

於是我開始想像我的叢林冒險，並且用一支彩色鉛筆成功地完成我人生的第一幅畫。我的一號作品，就像下面的這張圖：

我把這幅傑作拿給大人們看，還問他們有沒有被這張圖嚇到。

他們卻說：「嚇到？爲什麼會被帽子嚇到？」

我畫的根本不是帽子。明明是一隻蟒蛇正在消化牠吃進去的大象！於是我又畫了一張蟒蛇內部的透視圖，我想大人們應該就能看懂了。唉，大人總是需要清楚的解釋。

我的二號作品畫成像左頁這樣：

大人們這次看完的反應是叫我把這些蟒蛇圖，不管是外觀或透視的圖都丟掉，只要好好地學習地

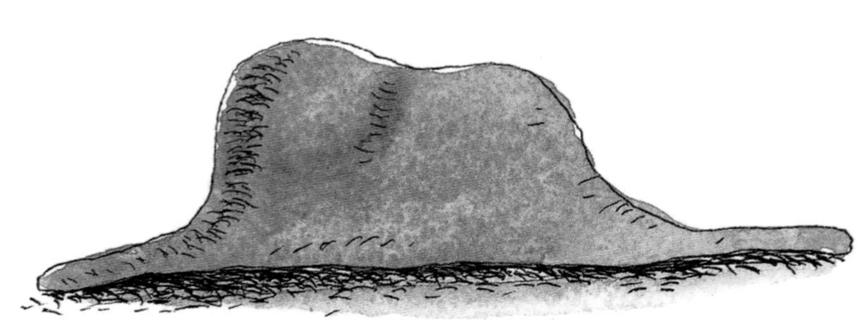

理、歷史、算術和文法就好。於是，我六歲那年，就放棄成爲畫家這個有趣的職業。我對一號作品和二號作品的失敗感到十分沮喪，大人從來都不靠自己去了解一些事情；而小孩老是要解釋給他們聽，眞的是好煩。

因此，我只好選擇另一個職業：學習開飛機。現在，我幾乎飛過全世界的國家，而以前唸的地理也眞的很有用，我一眼就可分辨出中國和美國亞歷桑納州的不同。這對如果在夜晚迷航的人來說，是個很可貴的經驗。

在這職業生涯裡，我跟很多嚴肅的人打交道過，花許多時間跟各種大人接觸，也曾經很仔細地觀察他們，但我對他們的印象並沒有多大的改變。

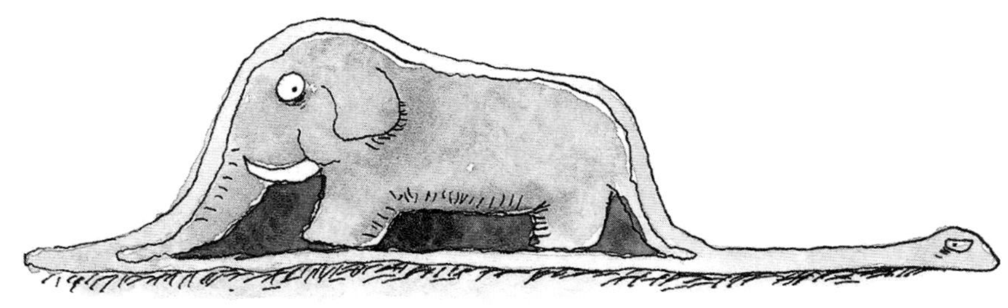

每當我遇到一個看起來似乎滿聰明的人，我就會給他看我那一直保存著的一號作品，這樣我就能知道對方是否是個有理解力的人。然而這些大人都說：「這是一頂帽子。」於是，我就不會再跟他解釋什麼蟒蛇、原始雨林，或星星了。我會遷就他們，談談橋牌、高爾夫球、政治，還有領帶等等的話題。這樣一來，這些大人就會非常高興他們遇到一個無所不談的人。

你覺得「大人」和「小孩」最大的不同之處是？

就這樣，我一個人孤獨地活著，因爲找不到眞正可以談心的人。然而六年前，我在撒哈拉沙漠發生的飛航意外，改變了一切。那次，我的飛機引擎出了點毛病，當時既沒有修理技師在旁邊，也沒有半個路人經過，我只好自己扛下這高難度的修復大任。這可是生死關頭：我的飲用水存量是撐不過八天的。

我在那裡的第一個晚上，想到要睡在方圓千里之內都渺無人跡的地方，就覺得，比一個因船難攀著浮木漂流海中的水手，還要孤立無援。

所以，你可以想像得到，第二天早上，當我被那個奇怪又微弱的聲音吵醒時，我有多驚訝了。那個聲音說：

「拜託——幫我畫一隻綿羊。」

「什麼！」

「幫我畫一隻綿羊。」

我像是被雷電擊中般跳了起來。我揉揉眼睛，看到一個十分奇特的小人，正睜大眼睛看著我。這裡有一張他的肖像，是我後來盡最大努力畫出來的。不過，他本人比這張畫更好看。畢竟，沒能將他傳神地畫下來並不是我的錯！我的繪畫能力早在我六歲時，就被那些大人們毀了，我除了畫過大蟒蛇的外觀和透視圖，再也沒畫過別的東西。

我目瞪口呆地站著，看著這個突然出現，如幻影般的人。別忘了，我現在迫降在這個方圓千里渺無人跡的沙漠。而眼前這個小人兒既不像是在沙漠裡迷路；也不像疲憊、飢餓、口渴或害怕的人，況且從他的身上一點兒都看不出他正迷失在這個沙漠。

當我終於回神說得出話來時，我問他：「你在這兒做什麼？」

他卻緩緩地重複著他所說的話，彷彿在說一件很重要的事，「拜託——幫我畫一隻綿羊……」

當一個人被某種神祕力量震懾住時，是絕對不敢不服從的。在四下罕無人跡，又面臨死亡威脅的情況下，我從口袋裡掏出一張紙和一枝筆，卻忽然想到我只學過地理、歷史、算術和文法這些科目，我（有些彆扭地）告訴這個小傢伙我不知道該怎麼畫。

他回答說：「沒關係，幫我畫一隻綿羊……」

可是我從沒畫過綿羊！於是，我就畫了一張以前畫過的蟒蛇外觀圖給他。然而，這小傢伙所說的話卻讓我大吃一驚。

「不是，不是，我不要蟒蛇把大象吃進去的圖。蟒蛇是一種危險的生物，大象又太大了。我是從很小的地方來的，那裡每樣東西都很小。我要的是一隻綿羊，幫我畫一隻綿羊……」

我只好再畫一張。他仔細地看了我的畫，然後說：「不行，這隻羊已經病得太嚴重了。再幫我畫一隻。」

於是我又畫了一張。

這次，他溫和且靦腆地笑。「你自己看，」他說，「畫上的動物不是綿羊。這是一隻公羊。牠頭上有角！」

於是我再重畫。但是這張也和先前那幾張的命運一樣，被拒絕了。

「這隻太老了！我要一隻可以活久一點的小綿羊。」

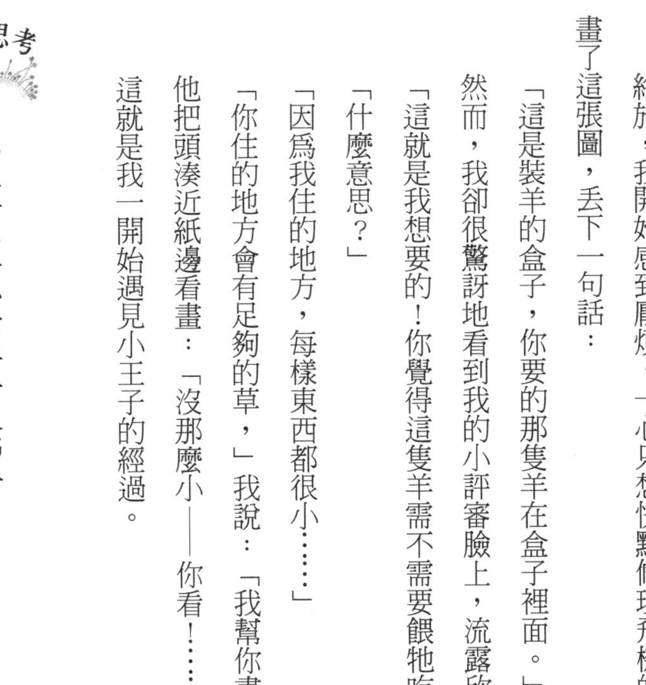

終於，我開始感到厭煩，一心只想快點修理飛機的引擎。我隨便畫了這張圖，丟下一句話：

「這是裝羊的盒子，你要的那隻羊在盒子裡面。」

然而，我卻很驚訝地看到我的小評審臉上，流露欣喜的光芒：

「這就是我想要的！你覺得這隻羊需不需要餵牠吃很多草呢？」

「什麼意思？」

「因爲我住的地方，每樣東西都很小……」

「你住的地方會有足夠的草，」我說：「我幫你畫了隻非常小的綿羊。」

他把頭湊近紙邊看畫：「沒那麼小——你看！……牠睡著了……」

這就是我一開始遇見小王子的經過。

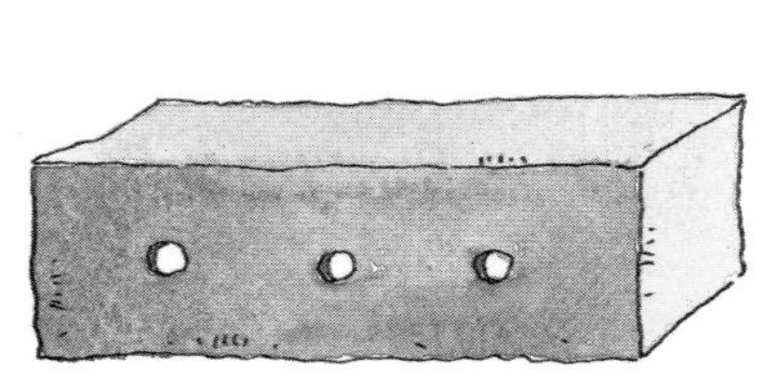

思考

小王子爲什麼需要一隻綿羊？

我花了很長一段時間，才知道他是從哪兒來的。小王子總是問我一大堆問題，但他對於我的提問卻好像聽不見似的，我只能從他偶然間說過的事，一點一滴地拼湊出眞相。

比如當他第一次看到我的飛機時，他問我：「那是什麼東西？」

「那不是『東西』。它會飛喔，那是飛機，是『我的』飛機。」

我很驕傲地告訴他，我可是一個飛行員。沒想到他馬上大叫：「什麼！你是從天上掉下來的？」

「是啊。」我謙虛地回答。

「哇！眞好玩！」小王子爆發出一連串笑聲，這使我有些火大。我希望他能以嚴肅的態度，來看待我的不幸。然而，他接著說：「那你也是從天上來的囉?!你來自哪一個星球？」

突然間，我想到他可能來自某個神祕的地方，我突然問他：「你也是從天上來的嗎?你是來自哪個星球？」

他沒有回答，只是盯著我的飛機，輕輕地搖頭：「顯然你搭的東西，不可能來自太遠的地方，對吧？」然後他就沈浸在自己的世界中。過了好一會兒，他從口袋裡掏出我畫的綿羊，像寶貝般仔細地看了一遍。

你可以想像得到，我對「另一個星球」這一知半解的訊息有多麼好奇，我想找到更多線索。

「小人兒，你是從哪裡來的?你住在哪裡?你要把我的羊帶去哪裡？」

他沉思了一會兒，然後回答：「你畫給我的盒子是最棒的，即使是晚上，我的羊

也能舒服的住在裡面。」

「當然囉！如果你人很不錯的話，我還可以幫你畫一條繩子，這樣白天你就可以把羊拴起來。喔，對了！還要一根柱子才行。」

小王子被這個想法嚇了一跳：「把牠拴起來？好奇怪的想法！」

「如果你不拴住牠，牠就會好奇地到處亂逛，然後就會走丟了。」

這個小人兒又再度笑了起來：「你覺得牠可以跑去哪兒？」

「哪裡都有可能啊。牠會一直向前跑。」

沒想到小王子憂鬱地說：「沒關係。我住的地方每樣東西都好小！」接著，他的語氣似乎透露一絲哀傷，「即使往前走，也走不了多遠……」

於是我有了第二個重大發現：小王子居住的星球，和一棟房子差不多大！

我一點也不感到驚訝。我知道，除了地球、木星、火星、金星等已經被命名的行星，還有數以百計的星球存在，有些星球甚至小到用望遠鏡都很難看見。當天文學家發現這種小行星時，就幫它編個號碼，當做它的名字。舉例來說，他可以把他發現的星球叫做「小行星325號」。

我有很充分的理由相信：小王子是來自小行星B–612。這顆小行星只在西元一九〇九年，被一位土耳其的天文學家透過望遠鏡看過一次。

當時，這位天文學家在發現這個星球後，在「國際天文學會議」上提出論點，但沒有人相信他的話，只因爲他穿的是土耳其的服裝。大人們都是這個樣子……

不過值得慶幸的是，爲了小行星B–612的聲譽，土耳其的統治者下令民眾都要改穿歐式服裝，違抗命令者就是死罪！當西元一九二〇年這位天文學家穿著光鮮亮麗的西裝，再一次發表演說，所有人都相信他說的話。

我之所以如此詳細說明小行星的事，包括它的編號，完全是因爲大人們的習慣。大人們喜歡數字。當你提到你交到新朋友時，他們從不會想知道那些眞正重要的事情，他們絕不會問說：「他的聲音好不好聽？他最喜歡什麼遊戲？他有沒有收集蝴蝶標本的習慣？」通常只是問：「他幾歲？他有幾個兄弟姊妹？他體重多重？他爸爸賺多少錢？」大人們總是覺得，只有這些數字才能幫助他們了解一個人。

假如你跟大人們說：「我看到一棟玫瑰色磚塊砌成的漂亮房子，窗戶上綴滿了天竺葵，鴿子們都棲息在屋頂上。」他們絕對對

那棟房子沒有任何想法。你必須說：「我看見一棟價值十億的房子。」他們就會大叫：「那一定是一棟很漂亮的房子！」

所以如果你對他們說：「小王子存在的證據是：他很討人喜歡、他很愛笑，而且他想要一隻羊。如果有人想要一隻羊，就可以證明他的存在。」他們只會聳聳肩，覺得你像個小孩一樣。但是如果你跟他們說：「他來自小行星B-612。」，他們就會相信，並且不會再用一些雜七雜八的問題煩你。

大人們就是這樣。你不可以跟他們作對，小孩子對大人們得非常容忍。

當然囉，我們這些很懂生命意義的人對數字根本不屑一顧。我想用童話故事的方式，開始敘述這個故事。我會這樣說：「很久很久以前，有一個小王子，住在一個沒比他自己大多少的小行星上；而且，他需要一個朋友……」

對於那些很懂生命意義的人來說，這個故事可以更接近真實的意義。

我不希望這本書變得無足輕重。對我來說，回憶這些事是十分痛苦的。自從我的朋友帶著他的羊離開，已經過了六年，我在這裡寫下他的故事，是因為我永遠不會忘

記他。忘記朋友是一件令人感傷的事，不是每個人都能有交心的朋友。況且如果我忘記他了，我就可能會變得跟那些除了數字之外，對什麼事都不感興趣的大人一樣……

由於這些想法，我買了幾枝鉛筆和一盒顏料。以我現在的年紀，很難重新開始畫圖——尤其自從六歲那年畫過大蟒蛇的外觀和透視圖以後。我還是會盡可能地畫得很像，但我不太確定是否算成功。也許有一張畫得還不錯，也許另一張就不行。而關於小王子的身高，我也犯了些錯誤，有的畫得太高，有的又畫得太矮；我也不太確定他衣服的顏色，只能憑記憶儘量東拼西湊原貌。我可能會在某些重要的細節上出錯，但你必須原諒我，因為我的朋友從來不對我解釋任何事，也許他以為我像他一樣，只可惜……我根本「不能」經由盒子透視裡面的羊。也許，大概是因為變老了，我有點像那些大人。

想像一下，你覺得小王子的聲音是什麼樣子？

每天我會透過我們偶然的談話，明白有關小王子居住的星球上的一些事情，以及他的離開、他的旅程。因此，第三天，我聽到關於猴麪包樹的危險性。

這次我得感謝綿羊的話題，因爲小王子突然被這個問題困住，很擔心地問我：

「綿羊眞的會吃灌木叢，對不對？」

「對啊！」

「喔！那太好了！」

我不明瞭爲什麼綿羊會吃灌木叢的事很重要，但是，小王子接著說：

「那麼牠們也吃猴麵包樹囉？」

我跟小王子說，猴麵包樹和灌木叢一點都不像，那是像教堂般高大的樹；而且，就算他帶著一群大象，這些大象連一棵猴麵包樹也沒辦法啃完。

一群大象這個想法讓小王子笑了。「那你必須把一隻隻大象疊起來……」接著他又說，

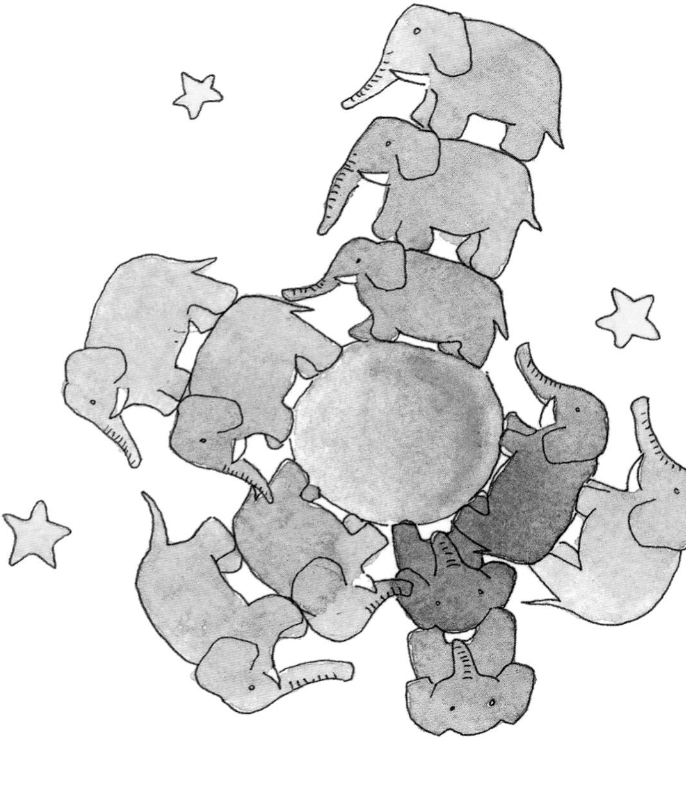

「猴麵包樹長成大樹之前，也是一棵小樹呀！」

「那倒是眞的。不過爲什麼要讓你的羊去吃猴麵包樹的幼苗呢？」

他說：「噢，這還要解釋啊。」他的口氣彷彿這是一個很簡單的問題，我卻必須聽到解釋才能理解。

原來小王子居住的星球就跟其他星球一樣，長著有益的植物和無益的植物，所以也就有好種子跟壞種子。然而種子是看不到的，因爲它們都很神祕地沉睡在地底，直到其中一顆想甦醒。剛開始時，這顆小種子會羞怯地伸伸懶腰，然後向著太陽長出嫩芽。如果長出來的是蘿蔔或玫瑰的嫩芽，就可以讓它們自由發展；如果是無益植物的芽，你就必須在辨認出來的當下，立刻把它拔除。

而小王子的星球上就有一些可怕的植物種子——那就是猴麵包樹的種子。它們密布星球各地的土壤裡，一旦它們佔有地盤，就不可能把它們除掉，猴麵包樹會將根鑽入泥土，接管整個星球。更別說如果星球太小而猴麵包樹太多的話，那些樹就會把星球擠爆……

「這是自律的問題，」小王子後來告訴我，「早上盥洗後，我必須很小心爲我的星球做晨間的清理——拔掉猴麵包樹的嫩芽。因爲猴麵包樹的芽長得跟玫瑰的幼芽很像，所以我一旦看出它們和玫瑰的幼芽長得不一樣，就得立刻拔除它們，這工作雖然很無聊，卻相當簡單。」

有一天，他建議我，爲我星球的小孩畫一張漂亮的圖。「如果他們去旅行時可能會有用處，」他又說：「有時候，把工作拖到最後再做也沒關係，可是像猴麵包樹這麼危險的事，拖到最後一定會有大災難。我知道有一個行星上，住著一個懶傢伙，他根本就懶得管那三顆小種子……」

因此我依照小王子的建議，畫了懶傢伙居住的星球。我不喜歡說教，但對於猴麵

猴麵包樹

包樹的危險性我們瞭解得太少，對於一個漫遊小行星的人來說，那是很大的危險。

於是在這一生中，我第一次呼籲：「孩子們，小心猴麵包樹！」我眞的很努力地畫出這幅畫，這樣我就可以警告那些和我一樣的朋友，他們從來都不知道要對抗這種危險。

這張畫給我們的啓示值得我不厭其煩地這麼做。也許你會問，「爲什麼在這本書裡，找不出任何一張像猴麵包樹這樣，令人印象深刻的畫？」答案很簡單：我盡力了，即使沒有每一張都成功——只有在畫猴麵包樹的時候，我整個人才被一種急切的心情催促著。

思考

飛行員的星球有沒有猴麵包樹呢？

在第五天，我發現小王子生活的另一個祕密——再次感謝那隻羊。他突然問了我一個他心裡沉思已久的問題。

「羊會吃灌木叢，也會吃花嗎？」

「羊找到什麼就吃什麼。」

「有刺的花也吃嗎？」

「是啊，有刺的花也吃。」

「那麼那些刺有什麼用？」

我不知道。當時我正忙著將一個卡在引擎上的螺絲拆下來。飛機損壞的情形蠻嚴重的，而當我的飲用水也漸漸用光時，我開始害怕最糟的情況。

「那些刺有什麼用呢？」

小王子一旦提出疑問，就絕不放棄，而我正爲了螺絲生氣，於是不加思索地回答他：「刺一點用處也沒有。那是花朵用來表達恨意！」

「噢！」

安靜了一會兒之後，小王子不滿地說：「我不相信！花很嬌弱、很單純。她們會盡全力保護自己，她們認爲有刺會令人害怕……」

我沒有回答，那時自顧自地想：「如果這個螺絲轉不動的話，我就得拿一把槌子把它敲震出來。」

小王子又再次擾亂我的思緒：「所以，你想，花……」

「噢！不！」我大叫道：「不要！不要再問了！我什麼都不知道。我只是想到什麼就說什麼。你沒看到我正爲了重要的事在忙嗎？」

他瞪著我，愣住了。

「重要的事！」

他看著我，我正手握著榔頭，手指污黑地沾滿引擎油，蹲在他眼中看來醜得要命的東西面前……

「你跟那些大人沒什麼兩樣！」

我覺得有點慚愧。然而，他卻無情地繼續說：「你們把每件事都弄混亂……每件事都弄得亂七八糟……」

他氣極了，一頭金髮在風中擺動。

「我知道有顆星球住了一位紅臉紳士。他從沒聞過花香，也沒看過星星，更沒愛過別人。他除了算數以外，就沒做過別的事，他跟你一樣，整天不斷地說：『我正在忙重要的事。』而且，他還驕傲得要命！他根本就算不上是個人——他只是一個蘑菇！」

「一個什麼？」

「一個蘑菇！」

小王子氣得臉色發白。

「幾百萬年來，花朵生來就有刺；就像幾百萬年來羊都在吃花一樣。難道去瞭解花身上爲什麼會有這些沒用的刺，不重要嗎？花和羊之間的戰爭不重要嗎？這些事難道不比臃腫的紅臉紳士的數字更重要嗎？如果我知道——世界上唯一的一朵花，只長在我的星球上；而一隻羊卻在某天早上，一口就把她吃掉，而牠自己一點也不明白自己在做什麼——你居然覺得這不重要！」

他臉色漸漸轉紅，繼續說：「假如有人愛著一朵獨一無二，盛開在浩瀚星海裡的花，那當他抬頭仰望繁星時便會心滿意足。他可以告訴自己：『我心愛的花在那裡，就在那顆星球上……』但如果羊把花吃掉了，對他來說，所有的星光便會在剎那間消失了！而你竟然覺得這不重要！」

他說不下去，突然間流下淚來。

黑夜翩然而至，我放下手中的工具，槌子、螺絲、飢餓，甚至是死亡，對我都已不再重要。

在一顆星星，一顆星球，我的行星，地球上，有一位需要安慰的小王子。我將他擁入懷中，輕輕地搖晃他。我說：「你心愛的那朵花不會有危險，我幫你的羊畫個口罩；替你的花畫個護欄……我……」

我不知道該對他說些什麼，只覺得自己很笨拙。我不知道該如何才能和他一樣，不知道該如何再次與他交心。眼淚就是這麼奇妙的東西。

思考

玫瑰花爲什麼會有刺？

很快地，我對小王子說的那朵花瞭解得更多了。在小王子的星球上，花兒一向簡單，只有一圈花瓣；既不佔空間，也不會打擾任何人；清晨綻放於草地上，傍晚就凋謝。然而有一天，不知從哪裡來的一顆種子，小王子非常仔細地觀察它，因爲這株芽跟他以前看過的嫩芽都不一樣。

這可能是新品種的猴麵包樹。沒多久，這小株植物就停止生長，準備開花。小王子剛好看到這個巨形花苞長大，知道不尋常的事快發生了。這朵花仍舊在她綠色的身體裡裝扮自己，她精心挑選顏色，並逐一地調整花瓣的角度，她不想成爲一朵皺巴巴的罌粟花。她想開出整朵花苞的美麗。噢！是的！她是迷人的！她花了好幾天準備，然後某天早晨，就在日出之時，終於將她之前所隱藏的一切完全展現。

她經過這番精心的裝扮，並打著哈欠說：

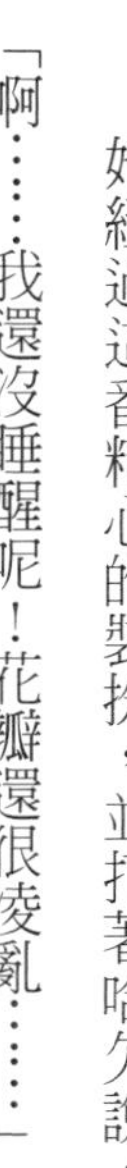

「啊……我還沒睡醒呢！花瓣還很凌亂……」

小王子發出少有的讚嘆：「妳好美！」

「可不是嘛？」花朵回答：「我還是和太陽同時出生的呢……」

小王子知道這朵花一點也不謙虛，可是她是多麼迷人哪！

「我想現在是早餐時間，」她補充道，「我在想，如果你夠仁慈，想到我的話——」

小王子慚愧地走了出去，替她提了一整壺水過來。

很快地，她虛榮心發作，並開始折磨小王子。

譬如有一天，她對小王子說：「我不怕老虎，更不怕牠們的爪子。」

「我的星球上沒有半隻老虎，」小王子回應，「而且老虎也不喜歡吃草。」

「我才不是草呢！」花朵溫柔地說。

「對不起……」

「我不怕老虎，不過我沒辦法忍受風。你可以準備屏風吧？」

「不能忍受風，對一株植物來說眞是不幸。」小王子內心想著，「就一朵花而言，她可眞難理解……」

「晚上的時候我想要待在玻璃罩裡。這個地方可眞冷，我從前住的地方——」

但她止話不再往下說，因爲她來到這時也只不過是顆種子，根本就不會知道其他地方。

這個愚蠢的謊言讓她感到很糗，於是她咳嗽了兩三聲，試圖轉移小王子的注意力。

「屏風呢？」

「我正要去找屏風，但是妳還在講話呀！」

於是她乾脆再多咳幾下，如此一來，小王子可能會感覺愧疚。

雖然小王子仍全心全意地關心花兒，但不久就不太相信她了。他把花朵無心的批評想得太嚴重，這使他變得很不快樂。

「我真不該聽她的話，」有一天，他告訴我：「不應該聽花說些什麼的，只要觀賞她們，聞聞花香就夠了。我的花使我整個星

球都滿溢香氣，可是我卻不會享受那美好。那個利爪的故事，反而讓我感到不安，我本來應該是充滿溫柔和憐憫……」

他對我傾吐祕密。

「我根本就不了解我的花！我應該看她的行爲，而不是聽她說的話。她的香氣讓我的生活更加多采多姿，我眞不該離開她的……我早該猜到，她那可笑小把戲背後的情感啊。花朵都是這麼自相矛盾！但我那時畢竟太年輕了，不知該如何去愛她。」

小王子的那朵玫瑰花是什麼個性呢？

我認爲小王子是利用候鳥遷移時逃走的。離開的那天早上，他便把星球上的一切東西整理得井然有序。他小心地清理活火山——他有兩座活火山，它們在他做早餐時很有用；他還有一座死火山，但是照小王子的想法，「誰也不知道會發生什麼事！」爲了預防萬一，他把死火山也清理了。如果火山被整理

得很乾淨，就會穩定且緩慢地燃燒，也不會突然就爆發。火山爆發和煙囪著火一樣。顯然在地球上，人類太渺小了，無法清理火山，這就是爲什麼火山常常爆發，爲我們帶來麻煩。

小王子那時帶著些許哀傷，拔起最後一根猴麵包樹的幼苗。他相信自己不會再回去了，在最後那個早晨，所有該做的例行公事，對他而言似乎都變得相當珍貴。當他最後一次爲花兒澆水，並且準備用玻璃罩罩住花兒的時候，他突然覺得好想哭。

「再見！」他對花兒說。

但是花兒沒有回話。

「再見！」他又說了一次。

花兒咳了一聲，但她並沒有感冒。

「我一直都很傻，」她終於開口了，「我覺得很抱歉。請你試著快樂起來好嗎？」

他覺得很驚訝，花兒竟然沒有罵他。他十分困惑，拿著玻璃罩站在那兒，他無法理解她這種冷靜的情緒。

「我是愛你的，眞的！」花兒告訴他：「你卻不知道。是我的錯……不過那不重要了。你一直都跟我一樣傻。快樂起來吧……把玻璃罩放到旁邊去，我不再需要它了。」

「那麼，風——」

「我還不至於那麼冷……夜裡的冷空氣對我有好處的，我是一朵花啊。」

「可是，動物——」

「哦，如果我想跟蝴蝶交朋友的話，當然就得忍受兩三隻毛毛蟲的拜訪囉。我聽說蝴蝶長得很漂亮。況且，如果沒有蝴蝶、沒有毛毛蟲，還會有誰來看我呢？你離我那麼遠……至於一些大型的動物，我才不怕呢，我有我的利爪啊。」

她天眞地展示了身上的四根刺，然後說：

「別再那樣傻傻地站著！既然你已經決定要走，就快走吧！」

因爲她不想讓小王子看到她哭泣。她是這樣一朵驕傲的花……

思考

小王子的那朵玫瑰花爲什麼是驕傲的花？

小王子發現自己的星球附近還有——小行星編號325，326，327，328，329，330，所以他開始一個一個拜訪它們，增廣見聞。

第一個小行星上住了一個國王。這位國王身著貴重的紫色貂皮長袍，坐在樣式簡單卻散發權威的寶座上。

「啊！來了一位子民！」國王看到小王子便如此大喊。

「他從沒見過我，怎麼會認得我？」小王子心想。

小王子不知道對國王來說，這個世界相當簡單，他將自己以外的人都當作子民。

「靠近一點，讓我好好把你看清楚點。」國王得意的說。他覺得自己終於成爲「某人」的國王了。

小王子四處張望著，想找地方坐下，然而整個星球都被國王那件巨大的貂皮長袍都蓋住了。所以，他只好繼續挺直站著。因爲很累，他便打了個呵欠。

「在國王面前打呵欠是相當失禮的。」國王說，

「我禁止打呵欠。」

小王子覺得很困惑，「我沒辦法停止呀！」他回答：「我長途跋涉來到這裡，睡眠不足……」

「噢，好，」國王說道。「那我就命令你打呵欠。我已經好久好久沒看過人打呵欠了。打呵欠可是很少見的。過來！再打個呵欠！這是命令。」

「這太爲難我了……我再也不會這樣了……」小王子非常難爲情地喃喃說。

「嗯！那麼……」國王回答，「我——我命令你有時打呵欠，有時——呃……」

國王結巴了，並且有些惱怒。因爲國王堅持他的權威必須受到尊重。他無法忍受別人抗命，不過他是如此和善，所以身爲一個統治者，他只下合理的命令。

「如果我命令一個將軍變成一隻海鳥，」他經常這樣解釋，「但他不聽我的命令，那並不是將軍的錯，而是我的錯。」

「我可以坐下嗎？」小王子怯怯地問。

「我命令你坐下。」國王回答道，把他威風的貂皮斗篷推到一邊。

然而，小王子覺得很疑惑……這個行星這麼小，國王能統治什麼？

「陛下，」小王子對國王說，「對不起，我想問問題——」

「我命令你問。」國王迅速地說。

「陛下，您統治什麼呢？」

「每一樣東西。」國王極爲英明且簡潔地回答。

「每一樣東西？」

國王比了個手勢，意思是他的行星、其他行星，及所有星球全都是。

「您比的全部都是？」小王子問道。

「我比的全部都是。」國王回答。

因爲他不僅是一位國王，還是一位宇宙的國王。

「那，星星也都聽命於您囉？」

「當然它們都聽我的，」國王說道，「而且是唯命是從！我不能忍受處罰這種事情。」

這樣的能力使小王子很驚訝。如果他能夠在同一天裡，不只看四十四次，而是看

七十二次，或者一百次，甚至是二百次夕陽——根本不用移動椅子的話。

當他想到他那顆被遺棄的小行星，小王子不覺哀傷起來。他鼓起勇氣，請求國王幫他一個忙。

「我想看夕陽……您可以命令太陽下山，讓我開心嗎？」

「如果我命令一個將軍從一朵花飛到另一朵花，像蝴蝶一樣；或是叫他寫齣悲劇；或是叫他變成一隻海鳥，而將軍卻不遵照命令的話，我跟將軍，是誰錯了？」

「是您錯了。」小王子簡短地回答。

「對！我們不應該要求別人去做他們能力以外的事情，」國王繼續說道，「權威的主要根據是合理。如果你下令叫子民去跳海，就會發生革命。我有權要求我的子民服從命令，因爲我的命令都是合理的。」

「那我的夕陽呢？」小王子提醒著，他從來不會忘記他提出的問題。

「你會得到你的夕陽！我會十分堅持這件事。但是，根據我政治學的知識判斷，我得等待適當的時機。」

「那會是什麼時候？」小王子問。

「呃！呃！」國王邊回答邊翻閱了一本巨大的年鑑。「讓我看看……那會是……大概……會是……今天晚上七點四十分左右。到時候你就可以親眼看到，萬物是如何遵從我的命令！」

小王子打了個呵欠。他很遺憾他將等不到夕陽，他已經感到有點無聊。

「在這裡我沒有別的事可做，」他對國王說：「我要走了。」

「不要走。」因為好不容易有了子民，而感到驕傲的國王說：「不要走，我可以讓你當上大臣。」

「什麼大臣？」

「司——司法大臣。」

「可是這裡沒有什麼人需要審判啊！」

「這可不一定，」國王說，「我還沒有遊遍我的領土呢！我年紀大了，這裡沒地方可以放馬車，走路又會讓我疲倦。」

「喔，可是我已經全看過了！」小王子邊說邊彎下身，瀏覽星球的另一側。「那邊也沒有半個人……」

「這樣的話……」國王回答：「那你就審判你自己好了。這可是最困難的。審判自己要比審判別人難得多。如果你能成功做好這件事，你就是一個具有眞正智慧的人。」

「您說得對，」小王子說：「但是我在哪都可以審判自己，沒必要留在這裡。」

「嗯！嗯！」國王說道，「我確信我的星球上住了一隻很老的老鼠，我晚上都會聽到牠的聲音。這樣吧，你可以審判牠呀！你可以每次都判牠死刑，牠的死活就看你如何審判。不過，每次你都必須再赦免牠，因爲這是唯一的一隻老鼠。」

「我不喜歡審判任何人，」小王子說：「我該走了。」

國王大叫：「不！」

小王子不想傷老國王的心，所以當他準備離開時，他告訴國王：「如果陛下要我立刻奉命行事，您可以下達一個合理的命令，像是——您下令我在一秒鐘內離開；而這種情況是最好的……」

國王沒有回話，小王子嘆口氣，遲疑了一下，然後離開了。

「我會封你為大使！」國王趕緊在他的後面大喊。

國王擺出一副很權威的模樣。

「大人們眞的很奇怪。」在他的旅程中，小王子這樣想著。

小王子求國王命令太陽下山合理嗎？如果不合理，是誰的錯呢？

在第二個行星上，住了一個驕傲自大的男人。

「啊！太好了！有位崇拜者來拜訪我了！」當他一看到小王子時，就開始大聲嚷嚷。

對於驕傲自大的人來說，除了他以外的其他人都是崇拜者。

「早安！」小王子說：「你戴的帽子好奇怪！」

「這是爲了答謝別人的稱讚。」驕傲自大的人說，「當人們鼓掌時，我就會脫帽致意。不幸的是，從來沒有人經過這裡。」

「噢！」小王子說。他不懂這個男人在講些什麼。

「快點拍手。」驕傲自大的人說。

小王子於是拍手；然後這個驕傲自大的男人就脫下帽子，謙虛地鞠躬。

「這比先前拜訪的那位國王好玩多了。」小王子又多拍了幾次手。驕傲自大的男人也再度脫帽致意。

玩了五分鐘後，小王子開始厭倦這個無聊的遊戲。

「要怎麼做，你的帽子才會掉下來？」小王子問。

但這個驕傲自大的人沒有回應，驕傲自大的人只聽得見讚美。

「你眞的很崇拜我嗎？」他問小王子。

「崇拜是什麼意思？」

「崇拜的意思，就是你認爲我是這個星球上最帥、穿得最漂亮、最有錢、而且最聰明的人……」

「可是，你的星球上就只有你啊！」

「你就幫我一個忙，崇拜我一下嘛。」

「噢！」小王子聳聳肩，「我崇拜你。」但小王子覺得這件事一點也不有趣。

所以，他離開了。

「大人還眞的是很奇怪！」他在旅程中如此想著。

崇拜爲什麼不有趣？

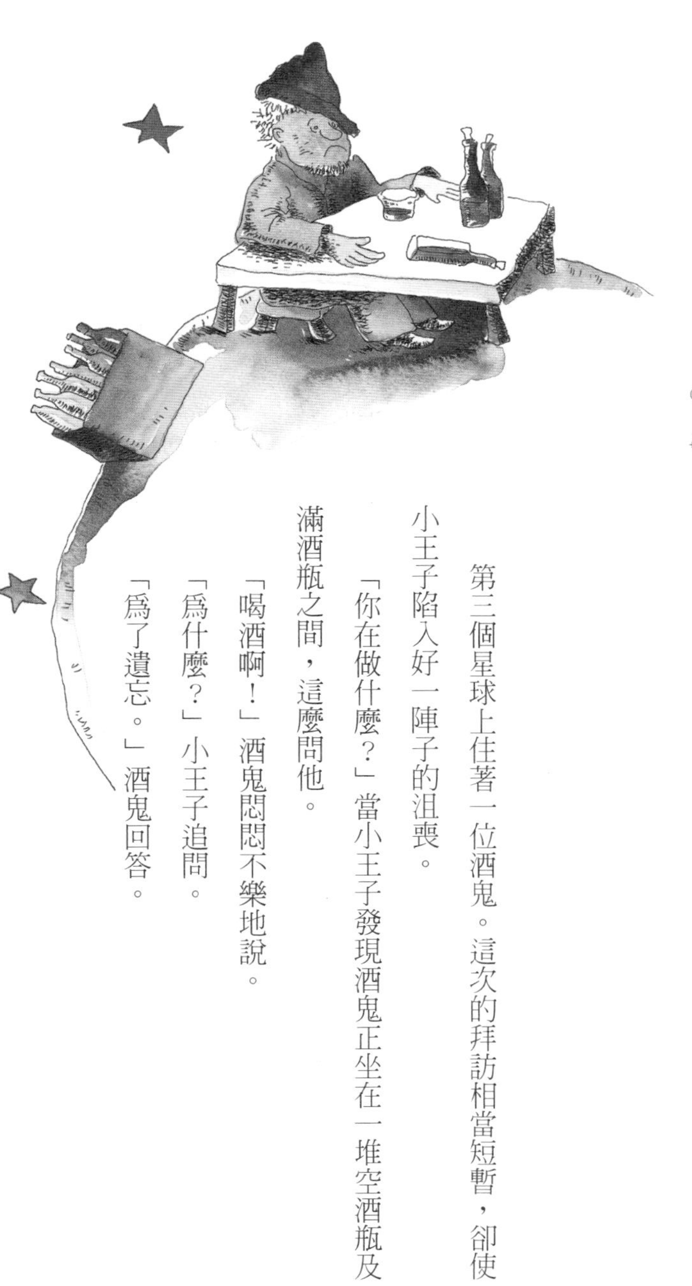

第三個星球上住著一位酒鬼。這次的拜訪相當短暫，卻使小王子陷入好一陣子的沮喪。

「你在做什麼？」當小王子發現酒鬼正坐在一堆空酒瓶及滿酒瓶之間，這麼問他。

「喝酒啊！」酒鬼悶悶不樂地說。

「爲什麼？」小王子追問。

「爲了遺忘。」酒鬼回答。

「遺忘什麼？」小王子問的當下都替他感到難過了。

「為了遺忘我很可恥。」酒鬼垂頭懺悔著。

「為什麼可恥？」小王子覺得他需要幫助。

「因為我喝酒！」酒鬼一說完，就醉倒在一片寂靜中。

小王子帶著滿心的困惑離開。

「大人們眞是非常、非常的奇怪。」他在旅程中這樣想著。

為什麼小王子覺得酒鬼奇怪？

第四個星球是屬於一個商人的。這個商人相當忙碌，忙到連小王子抵達時，頭也沒抬一下。

「早安，」小王子和他打招呼：「你的香煙熄了。」

「三加二等於五；五加七等於十二；十二加三等於十五。早安！十五加七等於二十二；二十二加六等於二十八。我沒時間再點煙了。二十六加五等於三十一。哇！總共是五億零一百六十二萬二千七百三十一。」

「五億什麼？」小王子問。

「什麼？你怎麼還在這？五億零一百萬──呃……我忘了。我不能停下來……我很忙！我只關心重要的事。二加五等於七……」

「五億零一百萬什麼？」小王子重覆道。只要他問了問題，就絕對不放棄。

商人抬起頭。

「我在這行星住了五十四年，這中間只被打斷過三次。第一次是二十二年前，不曉得從哪來了一隻甲蟲，發出惱人

的噪音，害我算錯四次。第二次是十一年前，我的風濕病發作。都怪我運動量不夠，也沒時間散步。第三次──嗯，就是現在！我剛剛說到哪裡了？五億零一百萬──」

「五億零一百萬什麼？」

這個商人突然意識到他如果不回答，就不可能得到寧靜。

「那些小東西，就是你常在天空看到的那些。」

「蒼蠅嗎？」

「蜜蜂嗎？」

「不，不是，就是小小的發光物。」

「噢，不是。就是小小的、金光閃閃的東西，那些讓懶惰人做白日夢的東西。不過，我只能關心重要的事情，我才沒時間做白日夢！」

「哦！你是指星星？」

「對！就是星星。」

「你爲什麼要五億顆星星？」

「是五億零一百六十二萬二千七百三十一顆星星。我可是相當關心重要的事，所以計算結果是非常精確的。」

「那你要這些星星做什麼用？」

「這些星星做什麼用？」

「對啊。」

「沒怎麼用啊。我擁有它們。」

「哦，你擁有這些星星？」

「是啊。」

「可是，我剛遇到一個國王，他——」

「國王並沒有擁有權，國王統治它們，這是不一樣的意思！」

「可是，你擁有這些星星有什麼用呢？」

「它讓我變得很有錢。」

「有錢有什麼用？」

「那我就可以買更多星星，只要有新的星星被發現的話。」

「這個人的邏輯跟那個酒鬼一樣……」小王子心想。

但是不管如何，小王子還是有其他問題：「人怎麼能擁有星星呢？」

「那還有誰可以擁有它們？」商人焦躁地反駁。

「我不知道，沒有人吧?!」

「那就對了！它們就是我的，因爲我是第一個想擁有它們的人。」

「這樣就可以嗎？」

「當然。如果你發現一顆沒有主人的鑽石，它就是你的；當你發現一座無人小島，那座島就是你的；當你比別人早一點想到任何創意，然後去申請專利，那就是你的。現在這些星星歸我所有，因爲之前從來沒人想過要擁有星星！」

「你說得很有道理。」小王子說道。「那要用它們做什麼呢？」

「我管理它們。」商人回答，「我正在重覆計算它們的數量。這相當困難，不過我是只關心重要事情的人。」

小王子仍然不滿意。

「如果我有一條圍巾，我就會把它圍在脖子上；如果我有一朵花，我可以把它摘下來帶走。可是，你不能把星星摘下來……」

「是不行，但是，我可以把它們放在銀行。」

「那是什麼意思？」

「意思就是，我可以把我有多少星星的數字寫在一張紙上，然後把這張紙鎖在抽屜裡。」

「這樣就好了嗎？」

「這樣就可以了。」商人說道。

「眞好玩。」小王子想。「這樣做甚至有點詩意，卻一點也不重要嘛。」小王子對於什麼事情是重要的，跟大人們的觀點非常不一樣。

他繼續對商人說：「我自己擁有一朵花，我每天幫她澆水；我有三座火山，我每個禮拜都會清理一次，我也清理死火山，以防萬一。對我的花和火山來說，被我擁有

是有好處的。可是，你對星星來說似乎沒有用處……」

商人張大嘴巴，卻想不到可以說什麼，然後小王子就走了。

「大人們眞的非常奇怪。」小王子單純地這樣想著，繼續他的旅程。

思考

爲什麼小王子會說商人只是個蘑菇？

第五顆星球眞的是很奇特。它是所有星球中最小的，只有容納一支燈柱和一位點燈夫的空間。

小王子無法理解，在宇宙裡，一個沒人居住也沒有房子的星球上，爲什麼需要燈柱和點燈夫？然而，他告訴自己：

「這個點燈夫也許很不尋常，但比起國王、驕傲自大的人、商人及酒鬼好多了。至少他的工作有意義。當他點亮街燈時，就好像賦予一顆星星或花朵一個生命一樣；當他熄掉街燈時，就像是送星星或花朵回去安眠。這是個美好又有用的工作。」

他懷著崇敬點燈夫的心情，登上這個星球。

「早安，爲什麼你剛剛把燈熄掉了呢？」

「這是規則，」點燈夫回答：「早安。」

「你的規則是什麼？」

「把燈熄掉！晚安。」點燈夫再次把燈點亮。

「可是，爲什麼你剛剛又把燈點亮？」

「規則呀。」點燈夫回答。

「我不懂。」小王子說道。

「沒什麼好懂的，」點燈夫說：「規則就是規則。早安。」

於是，他再次把燈熄了。

接著他用一條紅格紋手帕擦擦額頭。

「我這個工作眞的很辛苦。以前很合理，我只要在早上把燈熄掉，傍晚再點上就好了。我有一整天的時間可以休息，一整晚的時間可以睡覺。」

「後來規則變了嗎？」

「規則沒變。」點燈夫回答。「問題就在這裡。星球運轉的速度愈來愈快，而規則卻沒變！」

「所以呢？」小王子問。

「所以現在這個星球一分鐘運轉一次，我眞的是一刻也不能休息！我得在一分鐘內點燈、熄燈！」

「眞有趣！你的一天只維持一分鐘而已。」

「一點都不有趣！」點燈夫說道。「我們已經對談一個月了。」

「我們嗎？」

「對啊，一個月、三十分鐘、三十天了，晚安。」

點燈夫又把燈點亮。

小王子看著點燈夫如此忠於自己的工作，眞心地喜歡他。小王子想起自己以前只要把椅子往後挪就可以看到日落，於是他想幫助點燈夫。

「你知道嗎？」小王子說，「有一個方法可以讓你休息，當你想休息的時候……」

「我一直都想休息。」點燈夫說：「一個人是不可能同時努力工作又偷懶的。」

小王子繼續說：「你的星球這麼小，只要走三步就可以繞一圈，所以你必須走慢點，停留在陽光下就好了；當你想休息時你可以開始走路，想要白天有多長就有多長。」

「那對我來說沒什麼用，」點燈夫說，「我這一生中最愛的是睡覺。」

「你可眞是不幸。」小王子說。

「是啊，」燈夫說，「早安。」他把燈熄掉。

小王子繼續踏上他的旅程，他獨自想著：「國王、驕傲自大的人、酒鬼、商人一定都會看不起點燈夫。然而，他卻是我唯一不覺得他愚蠢的人。也許因爲他是唯一不爲自己而忙碌的人吧！」

他感慨地嘆了口氣，再度自言自語：「他是唯一一個我想跟他做朋友的人。可他的行星實在太小了，根本沒地方給兩個人站……」

然而，小王子卻不敢承認，他對於離開這個星球，感到特別難過的原因——這個星球上每二十四小時有一千四百四十次夕陽。

點燈夫的星球爲什麼愈轉愈快？

第六個星球是上個星球的十倍大。這裡住著一位老先生，他正在寫一本很厚重的書。

「哇！探險家來了！」當他看到小王子時，不由得大叫。

小王子氣喘吁吁地在桌子面前坐下，他走得有點遠了。

「你從哪兒來？」老先生問道。

「那本厚厚的書是什麼呢？」小王子問：「你在做什麼？」

「我是一名地理學家。」老先生回答。

「地理學家是什麼？」

「地理學家就是一個了解海洋、河川、城鎮、山脈及沙漠等位置的專家。」

「眞有趣，」小王子說：「終於有一個專家了。」他開始環顧地理學家的星球，發現這是他看過最宏偉的星球。

「你的星球眞是漂亮，有海洋嗎？」

「我不知道。」地理學家說道。

「哦！」小王子：「那有山脈嗎？」

「我不知道。」地理學家回答。

「那城市、河流、沙漠呢？」

「這些我都不知道。」

「但你是一名地理學家啊！」

「是啊，」地理學家說道，「但我不是探險家啊。我這兒根本沒有探險家。地理學家是不需要去計算和探測城鎮、河流、高山、大海、大洋、沙漠的。地理學家的工作太重要了，根本不能在外面閒晃！他是絕不能離開書桌的，不過，他會從探險家那兒接收資訊做爲研究材料。他會問他們問題，記錄他們的經歷。要是某位探險家提供的旅遊記錄過分有趣，那地理學家就會調查他的品行。」

「爲什麼？」

「一名說謊探險家會讓地理學家寫的書變糟！飲酒過量的探險家也是一樣。」

「爲什麼？」

「因爲酒醉的人會看到雙重影像啊。所以地理學家會把原本只有一座山的地方標示成兩座。」

「我認識一個人，他可能就是這種探險家。」小王子說。

「可能是這樣。所以如果一個探險家的品行似乎還不錯，他的發現就得好好地調查一番。」

「你會跑去那些地方察看嗎？」

「不，那太複雜了。可以要求探險家必須提出一些證據。譬如，探險家發現一座大山，他就得把山上的大石頭搬回來才行。」

地理學家突然變得興奮。

「不過——你來自遙遠的地方！你是探險家！你必須描述你的行星給我聽！」

地理學家打開他的紀錄冊，削尖他的鉛筆。

「探險家的敘述一開始是用鉛筆寫，等探險家把證據帶回來以後，才會用鋼筆寫下來。」

「說吧！」地理學期待地問。

「噢，我住的地方不是很有趣，」小王子說，「它很小。我有三座火山——兩座活火山、一座死火山，雖然不知道它會不會再次爆發。」

「你當然不會知道。」地理學家說。

「我還有一朵花。」

「我們對花不感興趣。」地理學家說。

「爲什麼？那是我的星球上最美的東西啊！」

「因爲花不列入記錄，」地理學家說，「因爲花朵是『朝生暮死』的。」

「什麼是『朝生暮死』？」

「地理學書籍是所有事物中最重要的，」地理學家說道，「它們永遠不會褪流行。一座山幾乎不太會移動；而海洋也不太可能乾涸，我們記載的是永恆的事物。」

「可是，死火山也可能再度活起來啊，」小王子問：「『朝生暮死』是什麼意思？」

「對我們來說，不論死火山或活火山都一樣。」地理學家說道。「我們在意的只是山，而山是不會移動的。」

「但是，『朝生暮死』是什麼意思？」小王子又問。在他一生中，只要他開始問問題就不會放棄。

「就是『註定很快消失』的意思。」

「我的花註定很快消失？」

「那當然。」

「我的花是朝生暮死的，」小王子心想，「而且她只有四根刺保護自己、對抗外界。我竟然將她獨自留在星球！」

這是小王子第一次對自己的離開感到懊悔；不過，他很快地再次振奮精神。

「你建議我下一站去哪兒呢？」他問。

「地球，」地理學家回答：「它的名聲不錯。」

於是小王子離開了，心中想念著他的花。

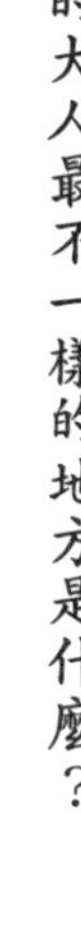

地理學家和前面五個星球的大人最不一樣的地方是什麼？

地球真不是一個普通的星球！有一百一十一位國王（當然，也包括黑人國王在內）、七千位地理學家、九十萬個商人、七百五十萬個酒鬼，還有三億一千一百萬個驕傲自大的人——這些全部加起來，大約有二十億個大人。

爲了讓你對地球的大小有概念，我可以告訴你，在發明電燈之前，如果要點亮全球六大洲的話，就得勞動四十六萬二千五百一十一個點燈夫來點燈。

從遠方看，這會是相當壯觀的場面。這群點燈大隊的動作排列大概會和芭蕾舞一樣整齊。

首先上場點燈的應該是紐西蘭和澳洲的點燈夫，點完燈便退回去，睡覺；接著，就換中國和西伯利亞的點燈夫，從大隊中出場，接著很快就退回去；然後輪到蘇俄和印度的點燈夫；隨後是非洲和歐洲；再來是南美洲和北美洲的點燈夫。而且不會有人弄錯出場的順序，這眞是一個奇觀啊！

唯一可以過得比較輕鬆的點燈夫，只有負責北極孤燈和南極孤燈的點燈夫，他們一年只要工作兩次就可以了。

思考

南北極的點燈夫爲什麼一年只要工作兩次？

當你試著想詼諧一點說故事時，就會發現你自己會撒點無關緊要的小謊。我並沒有完全眞實地告訴你點燈夫的事。我可能會讓那些不清楚地球現狀的人，留下錯誤的印象。人們在地球上所佔據的空間其實很小；如果將地球上二十億人像參加聚會般緊密地排在一起，他們很容易就能擠進一個邊長三十二公里的正方形廣場。所有人類都能擠進一個太平洋的小島。

你跟大人們說這件事他們絕對不相信。他們覺得自己佔了很大的空間，以爲自己跟猴麵包樹一樣重要。你可以告訴他們重要的事就是計算數字。他們喜歡數字，也樂在其中。但可別特別花時間做這件事，這一點也沒有必要。你可以相信我。

小王子一登陸就很驚訝，因爲他沒看到任何人。當一個月光色的東西在沙間移動時，他已經在猜：自己是不是登陸錯星球了。

「晚安。」小王子並不指望得到回答。

「晚安。」蛇說。

「我在哪一個星球？」小王子問。

「在地球上、在非洲。」蛇回答。

「哦！地球上難道沒有人嗎？」

「這是沙漠，沙漠中是沒有人的。地球是很大的。」蛇說。

小王子在一個石頭上坐下來，仰望天空。

「我在想，星星們閃閃發亮是不是爲了要讓每個人找得到自己的星球，」他說：「看看我的星球，它就在我們頭頂上，距離卻如此遙遠！」

「眞是個美麗的星球。」蛇說，「你爲什麼會來這裡？」

「我和一朵花之間有點問題。」小王子說。

「噢！」蛇說。

他們倆沈默了一會兒。

「所有的人都去哪兒了？」小王子再度開口：「在沙漠裡有點寂寞呢。」

「人群裡也會有寂寞的。」蛇說。

小王子凝視蛇很長一段時間。

「你是個有趣的生物。」他說，「只跟我的手指一樣粗……」

「可是，我比國王的手指頭還要有力。」蛇說。

小王子微笑了。

「你才沒有什麼力呢！你又沒有腳，也走不了多遠……」

「我可以帶你去比任何船都更遠的地方。」蛇說。

牠把自己纏在小王子的腳踝上，就像一只金鐲子一樣。

「地球上無論是誰被我碰到，就會被我送回老家，」牠繼續說，「可是，你是如此純潔，又來自某個星球……」

小王子沒有回答。

「我為你感到難過——在這個花崗岩組成的地球上，你是如此脆弱，」蛇說，「如果你發現自己很想家的話，我可以幫助你……」

「噢！我完全了解你的意思，」小王子說：「可是，為什麼你的話像是猜謎呢？」

「我專門解答謎題。」蛇說。

接著他倆陷入沈默。

思考

小王子明白蛇的什麼意思？

小王子穿越沙漠，但他只遇到一朵花。那是一朵有著三個花瓣，看起來很普通的花。

「早安。」小王子說。

「早安。」花說。

「人們都在哪？」小王子有禮貌地問。

這朵花曾看到一隊商隊經過。

「人嗎？大概有六、七個吧，我想我幾年前看過他們，但

是你找不到他們的。他們被風吹走了；你知道的，他們沒有根的，生活很艱困。」

「再見了。」小王子說。

「再見。」花兒說。

這朵花眞的看見過一隊商人被風吹走嗎？

之後，小王子爬上一座高山。以前他認識的山，就只有他那高到膝蓋左右的三座火山，他還很習慣把死火山當做小椅子呢！他心想，「登上這麼高的一座山，我就可以一眼望盡整個星球和所有人了……」

然而，他可以看見的僅有尖銳的山峰群。

「你好！」他並不指望有任何回應。

「你好——你好——你好……」一個回音傳來。

「你是誰？」小王子問。

「你是誰——你是誰——你是誰……」回音回答。

「做我的朋友吧！我好寂寞。」他說。

「我好寂寞——我好寂寞——我好寂寞……」回音回答。

「好奇怪的星球！」小王子心想，「這裡又乾、又粗糙、又險惡，一點想像力都沒有，只會重覆別人對他們說的話……在我的星球上，我的花總是第一個說話……」

思考

是小王子寂寞還是回音寂寞？

然而，走過沙漠、岩地和雪地之後，小王子發現了一條路。所有的道路旁都會居住著人。

「你好。」他說。

他在一個玫瑰花園裡。

「你好。」玫瑰花們回答。

小王子凝視著她們，她們看起來都像是他的那一朵花。

「妳們是誰？」他驚訝地問。

「我們是玫瑰花呀。」玫瑰們說。

他覺得很傷心，他的花曾經告訴他，全宇宙只有她一朵玫瑰花。而光是這個花園裡就有五千朵玫瑰花，長得跟他的玫瑰花一模一樣！

「她一定會氣得要命，如果她看到這幅景像，」他心想，「她肯定會咳得很厲害，而且會裝出一副快死的樣子，以免被嘲笑。而我就得裝出照顧她的樣子——因為如果我不這樣做的話，她真的會羞憤而死……」

然後他對自己說：「我以為我很富有，因為我擁有一朵全宇宙獨一無二的花。當我所擁有的只是一朵普通的玫瑰花，三座高度及膝的火山，其中一座還可能永遠都是死火山……

這些根本就不能讓我成爲一個了不起的人……」

於是，小王子趴在草地上哭泣著。

小王子爲什麼想要成爲了不起的人？

此時，狐狸出現了。

「早安。」狐狸說。

「早安。」小王子習慣性地禮貌回答。當他轉過頭，卻什麼也沒看到。

「我在這，在蘋果樹下。」那個聲音說。

「你是誰？」小王子問，並且補充了一句，「你看起好漂亮。」

「我是一隻狐狸。」狐狸說道。

「和我一起玩吧！」小王子提議：「我現在心情很不好。」

「我不能和你玩，」狐狸回答：「因爲我還沒被馴服。」

「啊！對不起。」小王子說。

可是他想了一想，又問：「『馴服』是什麼意思？」

「原來你不是這裡的人。」狐狸說。「你在找什麼？」

「人類，」小王子說，「『馴服』是什麼意思？」

狐狸說：「人類有槍，而且會打獵，眞是討厭；他們也養雞，這是他們的優點。你在找雞嗎？」

「不是，」小王子說，「我在找朋友。

『馴服』是什麼意思？」

「就是常常被人們遺忘的事情，」狐狸說道，「它的意思是建立關係……」

「建立關係？」

「沒錯，」狐狸說：「對我而言，你只不過是個小男孩，就跟其他千百個小男孩一樣。而我不需要你，你也不需要我。對你而言，我只是隻狐狸而已，就跟其他千百隻狐狸一樣。不過如果你馴服我，我們將會需要彼此，對我而言，你將會是宇宙間獨一無二的。」

「我好像懂了……」小王子說，「有一朵花……我想她已經馴服我了……」

「很有可能，」狐狸說，「在地球上，任何事都會發生。」

「噢，這不是在地球上發生的事。」小王子說。

狐狸非常好奇：「在別的星球嗎？」

「是的。」

「那個星球有獵人嗎？」

「沒有。」

「哇，太棒了！那雞呢？」

「沒有。」

「果眞沒有十全十美的事。」狐狸歎了口氣。

但狐狸很快地又說：

「我的生活相當乏味，我獵捕雞，人類獵捕我，所有的雞都一樣，所有的人類也都一樣，所以我已經感到厭煩。假如你能馴服我，那我的生命就會充滿陽光，你的腳步聲會開始變得與衆不同。其他人的腳步聲會讓我迅速躲到地底下，你的腳步聲會如音樂般呼喚我離開洞穴。你看到那邊的麥田了嗎？我不吃麵包，小麥對我來說一點用處也沒有。麥田無法讓我聯想到任何事，那眞的很可悲。但是你有一頭金黃色的頭髮，假如你馴服我，那該有多棒啊！金黃色的麥子會讓我想起你，而我將會愛上聽風在麥穗間吹拂的聲音……」

狐狸停止說話，並且凝視著小王子。

「求求你——馴服我吧！」

「我很想，」小王子說，「可是我沒有太多時間。我想去交朋友，

還有瞭解許多事情。」

「你只能瞭解你所馴服的東西。」狐狸說。「人類不會花時間去瞭解事情，他們會在商店裡買現成的東西，只是沒有任何一家店有販賣友誼。所以人類不再有朋友了。如果你要一個朋友，就馴服我吧！」

「那我要做些什麼事？」小王子問。

「你必須要很有耐心。」狐狸回答。「首先，你必須在稍遠的地方坐下來，像那裡的草地上。我會從眼角餘光看你，而你不能說話。言語會導致誤解。然後每天，你可以坐靠近我一點……」

第二天，小王子來了。

「你在同一時間過來會比較好。」狐狸說，「如果你在下午四點拜訪我，那三點的時候，我就會開始覺得快樂，接下來我就會愈來愈快樂。四點的時候，我就已經開始煩躁擔心了，那麼我將會知道快樂的眞諦！如果你隨便在任何時間過來的話，我就不知道該怎麼在心裡做好迎接你的準備……一個人必須要有一些儀式。」

「什麼是儀式？」小王子問道。

「這是另一件經常被人們遺忘的事。」狐狸說。「儀式就是使某一天跟另一天有所不同，讓某一小時跟別的小時也有所不同的事。舉例來說，那些獵人有一種儀式，每週四他們都會和村裡的女孩跳舞，所以禮拜四就變得很特別，我會一直散步到葡萄園。如果獵人想在任何時候跳舞，所有的日子也就會變得一樣。我就不能休息了。」

因此當小王子馴服了狐狸，離別的時刻即將逼近——

「噢，天哪！」狐狸說，「我快哭了。」

「這是你的錯啊，」小王子說。「我不想傷害你，是你要我馴服你的……」

「對啊。」狐狸說。

「但是，你快哭出來了！」小王子說。

「對啊。」狐狸說。

「那你根本沒得到什麼好處！」

「不！我有得到好處，因爲現在我擁有麥子的顏色。」他接著說：「再去看看玫瑰花吧！你就會知道，你的玫瑰花是獨一無二的。再回來和我道別，我會告訴你一個祕密。」

於是，小王子離開去看玫瑰花。

「妳們一點兒也不像我的玫瑰。」他告訴她們，「妳們什麼也不是。沒有人馴服過妳們，妳們也沒馴服過任何人。妳們就和我第一次遇見狐狸一樣，牠曾經和其他千百隻狐狸相同，但現在牠是我的朋友了，而且牠是世界上獨一無二的狐狸。」

玫瑰們顯得不太高興。

「妳們很美，」他繼續說，「但是很空虛。沒有人會爲妳們而死，沒錯，一般路人可能會認爲我的玫瑰和妳們很像，但只要有她一朵就勝過妳們全部，因爲她是我灌溉的那朵玫瑰花。她是我放在玻璃罩裡，被我保護不被風吹襲，甚至爲她打死毛毛蟲（只留兩、三隻變成蝴蝶）的玫瑰。她是那朵我願意傾聽她發牢騷、吹噓、甚至沈默的那朵玫瑰。因爲，她是『我的』玫瑰。」

然後，小王子回到狐狸那裡。

「再見。」他說。

「再見。」狐狸說。「我的祕密——它很簡單：『只有用心才能眞的看見。眞正重要的東西肉眼是看不見的。』」

「眞正重要的東西肉眼是看不見的。」小王子重覆著狐狸的話，以防自己忘記。

「因爲你付出時間在妳的玫瑰花身上，所以她才會如此重要。」

「因爲我付出時間在我的玫瑰花身上……」小王子說著，以免自己忘記。

「人類已經忘記這個簡單的眞理。」狐狸說，「不過你不可以忘記，你必須對你馴服的所有東西負責。你必須對你的玫瑰花負責……」

「我必須對我的玫瑰花負責。」小王子反覆唸著這些話，這樣他才不會忘記。

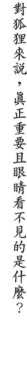

思考

對狐狸來說，眞正重要且眼睛看不見的是什麼？

「你好！」小王子說道。

「你好！」鐵路號誌員回應。

「你在這裡做什麼？」小王子問。

「我將旅客們分成一千個一批，」鐵路號誌員說，「再把帶他們上火車，往右邊或往左邊送走。」

一列光亮的火車發出雷聲般的隆隆巨響，極速通過，它的燈一閃一閃，有如一條銀色的蛇。

「他們眞忙啊。」小王子說，「他們要去哪裡呢？」

「恐怕連火車駕駛也不知道吧！」鐵路號誌員回答。

一列光亮的急速火車，也隆隆的從反方向進站。

「他們已經回來了嗎？」小王子又問。

「這是不同的一批人。」鐵路號誌員回答，「這裡是鐵路交叉點。」

「他們不喜歡自己住的地方嗎？」小王子再問。

「沒有人會安於自己所在的環境。」鐵路號誌員回應。

第三列火車的隆隆聲己經傳來。

「他們在追第一批旅客，對不對？」小王子繼續問。

「他們什麼人也不追。他們在裡面睡覺、打呵欠。」鐵路號誌員說，「除了小孩子會把鼻子壓在玻璃窗上。」

「只有小孩子才知道他們在找什麼。」小王子說，「他們會付出時間在一個娃娃身上，那個娃娃就會變得很重要。如果有人把娃娃拿走，他們就會哭了……」

「是啊，孩子眞幸運。」鐵路號誌員說道。

思考

鐵路號誌員說「孩子眞幸運。」是什麼意思？

「早安。」小王子說。

「早安。」商人說。

這個商人專賣一種止渴的藥丸。一個星期吃一顆，你就可以不必喝水。

「你爲什麼要賣這種藥丸呢？」小王子問。

「這種藥丸可以節省很多時間呀！」商人回答。「專家已經計算過，每星期可以節省五十三分鐘。」

「人們會怎麼運用那五十三分鐘？」

「他們愛怎麼用，就怎麼用。」

「如果我有空下來的五十三分鐘，」小王子說：「我會漫步到泉水邊。」

思考

人們為什麼需要多餘的時間？

這是我在沙漠飛機失事的第八天。當我正聽著小王子說商人的故事時，我也喝完我的最後一滴水。

「噢，」我告訴小王子，「聽你敘述的冒險是很棒。不過我還沒修好飛機，而且現在水也一滴不剩了；『如果』我可以，我很樂意散步到泉水邊！」

「我的朋友狐狸他——」小王子告訴我。

「孩子，你的那隻狐狸朋友，跟這件事沒什麼關係。」

「爲什麼？」

「因爲，我們就快要渴死了……」

他根本就不了解我的意思，於是繼續說：

「有個朋友很好，即使你快死了，像我就很高興，我『眞的』擁有一個狐狸朋友……」

「他根本一點危機意識也沒有。」我提醒自己，「他根本就沒有渴過，也沒餓過，他所需要的只是一點陽光就可以了。」

他凝視著我，回答了我正在思考的問題：

「我也很渴，我們去找井吧……」

我疲倦地聳聳肩；在廣袤無垠的沙漠裡，想找到一口井是不可能的。然而，我們還是出發了。

我們沈默地走了數小時以後，黑夜降臨，星星升起。

我渴得有些神智不清，乍看星空，彷彿自己正置身夢中。小王子說過的話在我腦海中迴盪——

「你也口渴嗎？」我說。

他沒有回答我的問題，他只說：「水對心靈很有用……」

我不了解他的意思，只好沈默。我知道，人類絕不可以對他產生質疑。

他累了，於是他坐下來。我也坐在他身旁。

過了一會兒，他說：

「因爲有一朵我們看不見的花，星星才顯得如此美麗。」

「嗯。」我默默地看著在月光下不斷綿延的沙堆。

「沙漠是如此的美麗。」小王子說。

這倒是眞的。我一直很喜歡沙漠。你可以坐在沙丘上，即使看不到任何東西，也聽不見任何聲音；無聲中卻有某種東西散發出光芒……

「沙漠是因什麼而美麗呢？」小王子說，「是因爲它不知在何處藏了一口井嗎？」

我相當驚訝，我突然理解他說的沙漠的神祕光芒，當我還小的時候，我住在一棟

古老的房子裡，傳說那裡埋有寶藏。當然，沒有人能找到寶藏，可能也沒有人看過寶藏。那房子卻因此籠罩著魔力。我家的地心深處，埋藏了一個祕密……

「對，」我對小王子說，「不管是房子、星星，或是沙漠——都因爲有看不見的東西而顯得美麗！」

「我很高興你同意我對狐狸的看法了。」他說。

當小王子沉浸夢中，我把他抱起來，再度出發。

我覺得很感動，彷彿我懷裡抱著一件易碎的珍寶。對我來說，世界上再也沒有比小王子更易碎的寶物了。

月光下，我看著他蒼白的額頭，緊閉的雙眼，微風中顫動的捲髮。我內心想：「我看到的不再是外觀而已，眞正重要的是那些看不到的東西……」

他的雙唇半開，形成了一個微笑。

我再次想：「我之所以會對小王子這麼感動，是因爲他對玫瑰花的忠誠——玫瑰的存在讓他發光，就像是點燃的燈火，即便是他睡著了……」

然後我覺得他似乎更易碎了。燈火需要保護，一陣狂風就可以將它們吹熄。於是，我繼續向前走，直到天亮，我找到了一口井。

思考

你曾看不見什麼而心碎過？

「人們拚命將自己擠進急速火車裡，」小王子說：「卻不知道自己在尋找什麼。於是他們變得憂慮煩躁，在原地打轉。」

然後他又補充道：「其實根本不值得……」

我們所找到的井不像沙漠的井。沙漠的井只是地上的洞，這個井卻像村莊的井。可是這四周並沒有村莊啊。我心想，我一定是在做夢……

「真奇怪，」我告訴小王子，「打水用具很齊全呢，滑輪、水桶、繩子。」

他笑了，拉起繩子，轉動滑輪。滑輪發出的聲音，如同被風吹動般的老舊風向標。

「你聽！」小王子說。「我們叫醒這口井了，它正在唱歌呢……」

我不希望小王子累死自己。

「讓我來吧！」我說，「這對你來說太重了。」

我慢慢地把水桶拉至我穩穩坐著的水井邊緣。滑輪的歌聲仍然在耳際迴響，而顫動的水面還閃爍著粼粼波光。

「我好渴，好想喝水，」小王子說，「給我一點兒水喝……」

我明白他在找尋什麼了。

我把水桶舉到他唇邊，他閉著眼睛啜飲，彷彿飲用饗宴上的酒。這時候水變得不是普通一般的水，它來自星空下漫步、滑輪的歌聲和我打水的辛勞呢！它就像是一件禮物，慰藉我的心靈。當我還是小男孩時，聖誕樹上的光、午夜彌撒的音樂及溫柔的笑臉，都爲我收到的禮物綻放出光芒。

「人類在一個花園裡種了五千朵玫瑰，」小王子說：「卻找不到眞正想要的。」

「是啊，他們是沒找到。」我回答。

「其實他們要找的東西可能存在一朵玫瑰和一口水中。」

「是啊，很有可能。」我說。

然後小王子接著說：

「雙眼是盲目的，我們必須用心體會才能看見。」

我已經喝過水，呼吸也順暢許多。旭日將沙漠染成蜂蜜色，我對這個顏色感到很快樂。然而，爲什麼我的心頭又是如此憂傷？

「你一定要遵守諾言。」小王子溫柔地說，他再度在我身旁坐下。

「什麼諾言？」

「你知道的——替我的羊畫口罩……我得對我的玫瑰花負責呀！」

我從口袋裡掏出我畫的草圖。小王子看看那些畫，然後笑著說：

「你的猴麵包樹看起來好像高麗菜。」

「喔！」

我本來是爲我畫的猴麵包樹感到相當驕傲的！

「你的狐狸耳朵畫得像角，而且它們太長了。」然後他又笑了。

「這不公平啊，我唯一會畫的就只有蟒蛇的外觀和透視圖。」

「噢，沒關係的，」他說，「小孩會看懂的。」

然後，我畫了一個口罩。當我把口罩交給他時，我的心跳似乎停止了。

「你有什麼計畫是我不知道的嗎？」

他沒有回答我，只說：

「你知道嗎，明天就是我到地球的週年紀念日了……」

經過短暫的沈默後，他繼續說：

「我降落的地方就在附近。」

然後他臉紅了。

再一次，不知道為什麼，我心頭又掠過一絲憂傷。突然間我想到一個問題：

「那一週前的早晨，我在罕無人跡的地方遇見你，並不是偶然？當時你準備回到你降落的地方？」

小王子的臉又紅了。

於是我有點猶豫地說：

「是因爲週年紀念日的關係嗎？」

小王子再一次臉紅了。他沒有回答我的問題。但臉紅就表示「是」了，不是嗎？

「噢，」我說：「我好怕。」

他卻回答：「現在，你必須要回去工作了，快回去修飛機吧。我會一直在這裡，你明天傍晚再回來這裡……」

可是我放不下心。我想起了狐狸的話，如果你讓自己被馴服，就有可能會流淚……

思考

飛行員明白小王子在追尋什麼嗎？

水井旁有一座老舊傾塌的石牆。

當我隔天晚上修理飛機後趕過來時，從遠處就看見小王子坐在牆上，兩隻腳晃來晃去。我聽到他說：

「你不記得了嗎，這裡不是正確地點。」

一定是誰在跟他說話，因爲那聲音回答：

「是，是！是今天沒錯，但這裡不是正確的地點。」

我繼續朝著牆走去，仍然沒看到或聽見任何人的聲音。

但是，小王子再度說話了。

「——當然。你可以在沙漠上找到我最初的足跡。在那兒等我吧！我今晚會在那裡。」

我距離那片牆只相隔二十公尺遠，我卻還是沒看到任何東西。

小王子沈默一會兒後，又開口了：

「你的毒液夠毒嗎？你確定不會讓我痛苦太久吧？」

我停住腳步，內心感到一陣刺痛。但我仍然無法理解他在說什麼。

「你走吧。」小王子說，「我要下來了。」

我低頭看向牆腳，嚇了一跳。我看到一條豎起身面對小王子的黃蛇，牠三十秒內就能讓人致命。我從口袋裡掏出左輪手槍，奔跑過去。蛇一聽見聲響，便溜進沙堆裡，就像一條潺流的小溪慢慢地游移，並帶著一絲金屬般聲響，溜進石縫中。

我到達牆邊時，剛好及時抱住小王子——他的臉色蒼白的像一張紙。

「這是怎麼回事？你怎麼在和蛇說話？」

我解開他習慣圍住的金色圍巾，用一塊溼布擦擦他的太陽穴，又給他喝了一些水。我不敢再問他任何問題了。

他憂傷地看著我，雙手圍著我的脖子。我感覺得到他的心跳聲，就像一隻遭受槍傷，垂死鳥兒般的心跳聲……

「我很高興你終於解決引擎的問題了。」他說，「現在你可以回家了——」

「你怎麼知道？」

我就是來告訴他，我修理引擎的工作順利地讓我不敢置信。

他沒有回答我的問題，接著說：

「我今天也要回家了……」

又悲傷地說：

「路途好遠……也比較困難……」

我內心知道，不尋常的事就要發生了。我像抱著孩子，緊緊地將他擁入懷裡。他似乎快一頭掉進無底的深淵裡，而我卻無法拉住他……

他的表情非常嚴肅，遙遠而迷茫。

「我有你的羊，羊的盒子，還有口罩……」

然後，他哀傷地笑了。

我等待了很長一段時間，終於看到他的臉漸漸恢復紅潤。

「可憐的小傢伙，」我告訴他，「你很害怕……」

他眞的很害怕，但他靜靜地笑了。

「今天晚上，我會更害怕……」

再一次，我的心，因爲這種無力感而覺得寒冷。

我知道，我絕對無法忍受今後再也聽不見他的笑聲。對我來說，他的笑聲就像沙漠中的泉水。

「小人兒，」我說，「我想再繼續聽到你的笑聲。」

可是他卻說：

「今晚就滿一年了……我的星球會在我一年前降落地點的正上方……」

「小人兒，求求你告訴我，蛇、見面的地方、還有星星，都只是一場惡夢，對不對？」

但是他並沒有回答我的問題，他說：

「眞正重要的東西——是看不見的……」

「對，我知道……」

「就像我的花一樣。如果你愛上了某個星球上的一朵花，那麼只要在夜晚仰望星空，就會覺得所有的星星都開出花朵……」

「沒錯……」

「就像水一樣。因爲滑輪和繩子，使得你讓我喝的水有如音樂一般。你記得嗎？它是如此甜美。」

「是的……」

「你將會在夜晚仰望星空，找尋我的星球。我住的那顆星球太小，我沒辦法指出來給你看，不過這樣反而更好。對你而言，我的星球只是衆多星星中的其中一顆，所以你就會看著所有星星，他們都會變成你的朋友。而且，現在我還要給你一個禮物……」

然後，他又笑了。

「噢，小人兒，親愛的小人兒！我多麼喜歡聽到你的笑聲！」

「對啊，這笑聲就是我的禮物。它就會像我們喝的水一樣……」

「什麼意思？」

「星星對每個人的意義是不一樣的。對旅行的人來說，星星可以指引方向；對有些人來說，星星只是一些小光點；對專家來說，星星是研究對象；對我遇到的商人來說，星星是金錢。然而，所有的星星都是沈默的。只有你的星星顯得特別不同。」

「你的意思是？」

「我會住在這其中的一顆星星上面，在某一顆星星上微笑著，每當夜晚你仰望星空時，就會像是看到所有的星星在微笑一樣！」

於是他繼續笑了。

「當你撫平你的悲傷時（每個人都會克服的），你就會是我永遠的朋友，你要跟我一起笑。有時候，當你爲了與我一同歡笑而打開窗戶時……你的朋友一定會因爲你看著天空微笑，而感到驚訝。到時候你就可以告訴他們，『沒錯，星星常讓我笑了！』然後他們就會認爲你瘋了。這是我給你的小小惡作劇……」

他再次笑了。

「這就像是我給你很多會笑的小鈴鐺，而不是小星星一樣……」

說完，他又笑了。然後他又變得嚴肅。

「聽著，今晚……不要來！」

「我不會留下你一個人的。」我說。

「那時候我看起會很痛苦，而且一副快死掉的樣子。事情看起來會像那樣，所以我不要你來，也不要你看……不要來……」

「我不會丟下你一個人的。」

可是他開始擔心。

「我告訴你——這是因爲蛇——你不能被牠咬到，蛇是壞東西，牠們咬你可能只是爲了好玩而已……」

「我不會丟下你一個人的。」

突然間，他平靜下來：

「嗯！牠應該沒有足夠的毒液可以咬第二口……」

那天晚上，我沒有看到他出發，因爲他一聲不響地走了。當我追上他時，他正迅速且堅定地向前走，他只是對我說：「噢！你來了……」

他握住我的手，看起來很憂心。

「你不該來的，你會很難過。看到我快死掉的樣子，即使那不是眞的。」

我沉默不語。

「你知道的……路途太遙遠了，我不能帶著這副軀殼呀，那太重了……」

我沉默不語。

「那只是一副老舊的空殼而已，你沒有必要爲老舊的空殼而哀傷的……」

我仍然沈默。

他有些洩氣，不過他又試圖振作：

「這將會很美好。你知道，我也會看著星星啊。所有星星都將會是帶有生鏽滑輪的井；所有星星都會流出水來讓我喝……」

我依舊沈默。

「那會很有趣！你會擁有五百萬個小鈴鐺，我會擁有五百萬口井……」

接著他也沈默了，因爲淚水布滿了他的臉……

「就是這裡，讓我自己走吧。」

他坐了下來，因爲感到害怕，他又說：

「你知道的……我必須對我的花負責。她是如此脆弱！如此天眞無邪！她只有那四根沒用的刺，可以保護自己，對抗外界……」

我也坐了下來，因爲我再也站不住了。

「現在——就這樣了……」

他又遲疑了一會兒。然後站起身往前踏了一步，我卻沒辦法移動。一道黃色的閃光接近他的腳踝，有一陣子他待在原地不動。沒有尖叫，他像一顆枯樹般輕輕地倒下。因爲沙地的關係，他倒下時一點聲音也沒有。

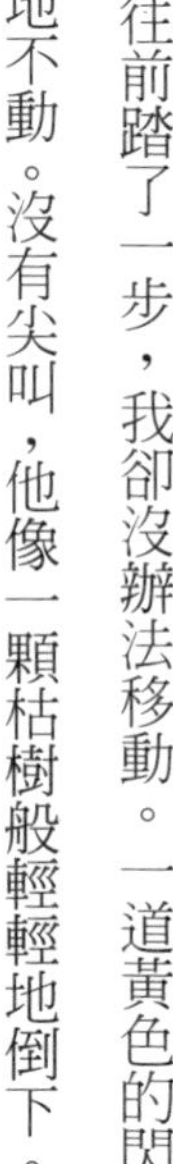

思考

你覺得飛行員曾馴服了小王子嗎？

如今已過了六年……

我一直沒有告訴別人這個故事。我的同伴都很高興地發現我還活著，我卻很難過，但也只是告訴他們：「我累了。」

現在，我的悲傷稍稍平息了，也就是說——還未完全平息。我確定，他是眞的回到他的星球了。因爲天亮時，我並沒有發現他的遺體。而他的身體其實並不怎麼重……在夜晚，我愛看星星，聽它們的聲音就像是聽見五億個小鈴鐺在響一樣……

不過，有一件極不尋常的事……當我幫小王子畫口罩時，我忘記畫口罩的鬆緊帶了。這樣他是永遠也無法把口罩套到羊的嘴上。所以我常常想：他的星球上發生了什麼事？也許羊眞的已經把花吃掉了……

偶爾我會想：「當然不會！小王子每晚都把玫瑰花放在玻璃罩裡，而且他會小心翼翼地看著他的羊……」然後我就會覺得很快樂，而所有的星星也跟著溫柔的笑了。

有時我又會想：「只要疏忽一下，後果就會很嚴重！萬一有天他忘記幫花蓋上玻璃罩，或者不小心讓羊跑了出來……」於是，所有的小鈴鐺就變成了眼淚……

這是一個謎題：對於喜愛小王子的你們來說——在某個地方，沒有人知道的某個地方，會不會有一隻我們不知道的羊，吃掉一朵玫瑰……世界會不會因此變得不同？抬頭仰望天空，問問你自己：羊是否已經吃掉那朵花了？然後，你就會看到世界萬物是如何地改變……

沒有大人會了解——這件事是多麼重要的事！

對我來說，這是世界上最美麗，也最令人哀傷的景像。這幅畫和前一幅畫是完全相同的。我又畫了一次，只是爲了讓你更了解而已。這就是小王子出現在地球上，消

失的地方。

仔細地看這幅畫，如果有一天你到非洲旅行，就可以在沙漠中再次認出這裡。如果你剛好經過，請你不要匆匆走過，在這顆星星底下稍待一會兒。如果出現了一個愛笑的小人兒走向你，如果他有著一頭金髮，而且從不回答問題，你將會知道他是誰。假若你心地善良，就不要讓我活在悲慘之中！請立刻寫信告訴我，告訴我：他回來了。

你覺得「大人」和「小孩」最大的不同之處是？

The Little Prince

★小王子中英雙語版

ANTOINE DE SAINT-EXUPERY

晨星出版

For Leon Werth

I hope that children will forgive me for writing this book in honor of a grown-up.

I have a very good excuse: this grown-up is my best friend in the world. I also have a second excuse: this grown-up understands everything, even books about children. My third excuse is this: this grown-up lives in France, where he is hungry and cold. He needs to be cheered up. If these reasons are not enough, then I will write this book in honor of the child from whom this grown-up grew. All grown-ups were once children. (But few grown-ups remember this.) And therefore I write this book:

To Leon Werth
when he was a little boy

Chapter I

When I was six years old, I saw a beautiful picture in a book. The book was called *True Stories From Nature*. The pictures showed a boa constrictor eating a wild animal. Here is the picture:

In the book it said, "boa constrictors eat their food whole, in one single bite. After eating, they cannot move because they must sleep for six months to digest the food."

✶✶✶✶✶✶✶✶✶✶✶✶✶✶✶✶✶✶✶✶✶✶✶✶✶✶✶✶✶✶✶✶

boa constrictor [ˋboə kənˋstrɪktɚ] ***n.*** 蟒蛇

✶✶✶✶✶✶✶✶✶✶✶✶✶✶✶✶✶✶✶✶✶✶✶✶✶✶✶✶✶✶✶✶

I thought about it for a while. And then, over the adventures of imagination, I drew my first picture with a colored pencil. My Drawing Number One, It looked like this:

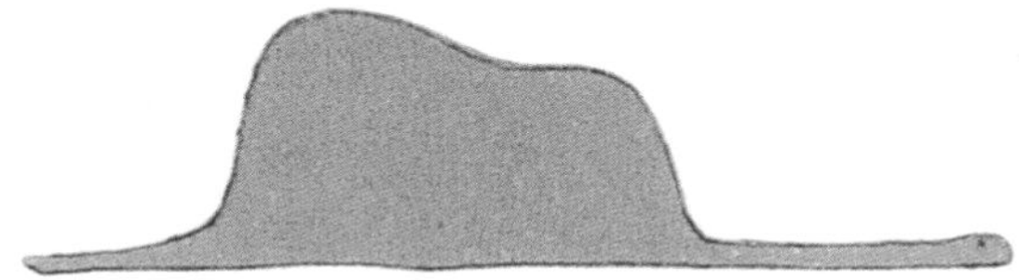

I showed my masterpiece to some grown-ups, and I asked them if my picture frightened them.

They replied: “Why would a hat frighten us?”

I didn’t draw a hat. My picture showed a boa constrictor that had eaten an elephant.

And then I drew another picture. To help the grownups understand, my second picture showed what it looked like inside the boa constrictor. Grown-ups always need to have things explained. My Drawing Number Two looked like this:

grown-up [gron ʌp] ***n.*** 大人們

The grown-ups told me to stop drawing boa constrictors, whether from the inside or the outside.

They told me to learn math, history, and geography instead. That is why, at the age of six, I gave up my dream of becoming a painter. I gave it up because of the failure of the two pictures. Grown-ups never truly try to understand, and children get tired of explaining things to them over and over again.

Instead of becoming a painter, I learned to fly airplanes. I have flown almost all over the world. It is true that studying geography is very useful. I can tell China from Arizona at a single glance. This kind of knowledge is quite helpful when you are lost at night.

* *

geography [ˋdʒɪˋɑgrəfɪ] ***n.*** 地理
useful [ˋjusfəl] ***adj.*** 有用

* *

Living among grown-ups for a long time, I have met many serious people in my life. I have spent a lot of time observing them, and my impression of them has not changed.

Whenever I met one who seemed intelligent, I showed them Drawing Number One. I wanted to see whether he or she understood. However, the grown- ups always answered:

"That is a hat."

Therefore, I would not talk about boa constrictors, wild animals or stars. Instead, I talked about things that interest them such as golf, politics, and clothing. And they would think I was a learned man.

* *

instead [ɪn`stɛd] ***adv.*** 反而

* *

Chapter 2

For years I have been lonely. I have met no one I could really talk to, until I had an accident with my plane in the Sahara Desert six years ago. I was all alone. I knew that I had to repair my plane by myself, without any help. It was a question of life or death for me: I had scarcely enough drinking water to last a week.

On the first night in the desert, I slept on the sand. I was a thousand miles away from anyone or anywhere. I was more isolated than a shipwrecked sailor on a raft in the middle of the ocean. So you can imagine my amazement when a strange little voice woke me up early in the morning. The voice said:

"Please… draw me a sheep!"

Sahara Desert [sə`hɑrə`dɛzɚt] *n.* 撒哈拉沙漠
draw [drɔ] *v.* 畫
sheep [ʃip] *n.* 綿羊

"What!"

"Draw me a sheep..."

I jumped to my feet, completely thunderstruck. And I saw a most extraordinary little man looking at me.

Here you may see the best portrait that I was able to make of him later. But my drawing is far from perfection. The grown-ups made me stop drawing at the age of six, and I never learned to draw anything except boas from the outside and boas from the inside.

Now I looked at this little boy in astonishment. I remembered that I had crashed in the desert a thousand miles away from anyone or anywhere. But this little man did not seem to be lost, tired, hungry, or scared. He didn't look like a child lost in the middle of the desert at all. When I was finally

able to speak, I said to him:

"But… what are you doing here?"

Again he said,

"Please… draw me a sheep…"

Even though I was in danger of death, a mystery overpowered me and I couldn't refuse the little man's request. I reached into my pocket and took out a sheet of paper and a pen.

But then I thought of one thing: although I had learned many things at school, I did not know how to draw. I awkwardly told him so and he replied:

"That doesn't matter. Draw me a sheep."

Since I had never drawn a sheep, I drew him one of the two pictures I had drawn so often. It was the boa constrictor from the outside.

He looked at it and I was astounded to hear him say:

"No, no! I don't want a boa constrictor that has eaten an elephant. Boa constrictors are very dangerous, and elephants are too big. Where I live, everything is very small. I want a sheep. Draw me a sheep."

So I drew a sheep. He looked at it carefully and said:

"No! This sheep looks sick. Draw me another one."

So I drew another one. My new friend smiled and said:

"This isn't a sheep… It's a ram. It has horns."

I drew another picture, but he did not like it, either:

"This sheep is too old. I want a

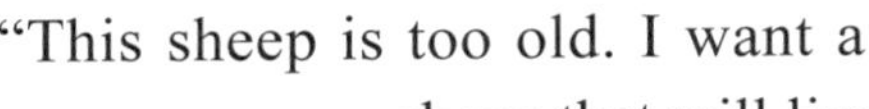

sheep that will live for a long time."

* *

elephant [`ɛləfənt] *n.* 大象

* *

By this time my patience was exhausted, because all I wanted to do is to repair my airplane. So I drew the picture below and told him:

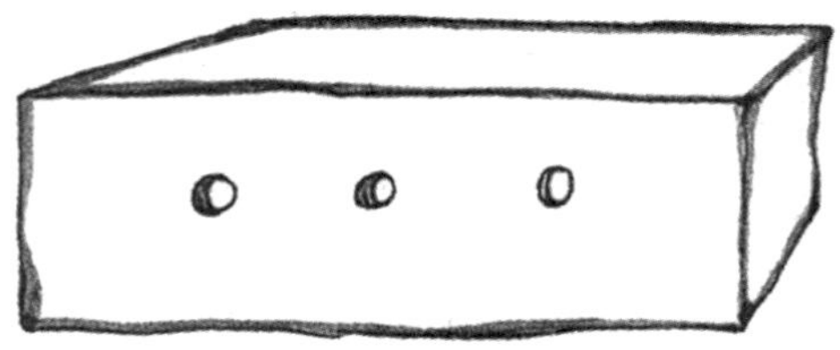

"This is a box. The sheep you want is inside."

I was surprised to see my little judge's face light up:

"That's exactly what I want! Do you think this sheep will need a lot of grass to eat?"

"Why?"

"Because where I come from, everything is very small."

"There will surely be enough grass for the sheep. I

* *

exactly [ɪgˋzæktlɪ] *adv.* 確切地，正好地

* *

gave you a very small sheep."

He looked closely at the drawing:

"Not so small, really… Look! He's fallen asleep…"

And that was how I first met the little prince.

chapter 3

It took a long time to find out where he came from. The little prince asked me so many questions, but never seemed to hear the ones I asked him. I could only learned about him through words he happened to say. When he saw my airplane for the first time (I shall not draw my airplane because that would be too difficult for me), he asked:

"What is that object?"

"That is not an object. It flies. It is an airplane. It is my airplane."

And I was proud to tell him that I could fly.

He cried out:

proud [praʊd] *adj.* 驕傲的，有自尊心的

"What? You fell from the sky?"

"Yes," I answered, modestly.

"Oh! That is funny…"

And the little prince broke into laughter, which I did not like. I want my problems treated seriously. Then he said:

"So you came from the sky too! Which planet are you from?"

At that moment, I seized the chance to get some information about the mystery of his presence. I asked him abruptly:

"So you came from another planet?"

But he did not respond. Then he said gently as he looked at my plane:

* *

funny [ˋfʌnɪ] ***adj.*** 有趣的
planet [ˋplænɪt] ***n.*** 行星
presence [ˋprɛzns] ***n.*** 存在

* *

"It's true that you could not come from very far away on that object…"

And he had not spoken for a long time. He took my drawing of a sheep out of his pocket and studied it quietly.

My curiosity was aroused by what he said, "other planets." I wanted to know more, so I asked him:

"Where did you come from, my little friend? Where is your home? Where do you want to take your sheep?"

After a while, he answered:

"It is good that you gave me a box for the sheep. At night he can use it as his house."

"Yes, of course, and if you are nice, I will draw you a rope to tie your sheep

* * * * * * * * * * * * *

tie [taɪ ʌp] *v.* 拴

* * * * * * * * * * * * *

up during the day. Oh yes, you will also need a post."

My offer seemed to shock the little prince.

"Tie him? What a strange idea!"

"But if you don't tie him, he will walk around. He may get lost."

My friend broke into laughter again.

"Where do you think he will go?"

"Anywhere. Straight ahead of him."

Depressingly, he said:

"That doesn't matter. Everything is so small where I live!"

And with a saddened voice, he added:

"Even if he went straight ahead, he couldn't go very far…"

chapter 4

I had just learned a second important piece of information: his planet was not much bigger than a house! That did not surprise me. Since there are large planets like the Earth, Jupiter, Mars and Venus, there are also hundreds of smaller ones. When an astronomer discovers one of these small planets, he give it a number instead of a name. He might call it, for example, Asteroid 325.

I had strong reasons to believe that the little prince was from a small planet called Asteroid B612. This

Jupiter [`dʒupətɚ] *n.* 木星
astronomer [ə`strɑnəmɚ] *n.* 天文學家們
asteroid [`æstə͵rɔɪd] *n.* 小行星

asteroid has been seen only once, in 1909, by a Turkish astronomer. The astronomer presented his discovery at the International Astronomical Congress, but nobody believed what he said because of his Turkish clothing. Grown-ups are like that.

Luckily for the reputation of Asteroid B612, a Turkish ruler made a law that all his subjects should change to European costumes or be penalized by death. The astronomer presented his discovery all over again in 1920. He wore a very beautiful suit and this time everyone believed him.

I told you the details of the asteroid and made

Turkish[ˋtɝkɪʃ] *adj.* 土耳其的
discovery [dɪsˋkʌvərɪ] *n.* 發現

a note of its number for you, all because of grown-ups.

Grown-ups love numbers. When you tell them about a new friend, they never ask important questions. They never ask: "What does his voice sound like? What games does he like best? Does he collect butterflies?"

Instead, they ask: "How old is he? How many brothers and sisters does he have? How much does he weigh? How much money do his parents make?" They think that they will know about him through these questions. If you say to grown-ups: "I saw a beautiful house made of red bricks with flowers in the windows..." they would not be able to picture the house. You have to tell them: "I saw a house that cost one hundred thousand francs." Then the grown-ups would say: "What a beautiful house!"

So, if you say to the grown-ups: "I know that the little prince is real because he was beautiful, he laughed, and he wanted a sheep. If someone wants a sheep, that proves he is real." They would not believe you and treat you like a child! But if you say: "He comes from Asteroid B612." Then the grown-ups would believe you, and they would stop asking questions. Grown-ups

are like that. You cannot hold it against them. Children should be forgiving to grown-ups.

But, of course, for us who understand life, numbers are nothing. I should have begun this book as a fairy tale. I should have written:

"Once upon a time there was a little prince. He lived on a planet that was not much bigger than he was, and he needed a sheep…" For those who understand life, that would have felt much truer.

No one should read my book carelessly. I have suffered too much grief in setting down these memories. It's been six years since my friend left with his sheep. If I try to describe him here, it is to make sure that I shall not forget him. To forget a friend is sad. Not everyone has had a friend. And if I forget him, I may become like the grown-ups who are no longer interested in anything but numbers...

It is hard to start drawing again at my age. I have not drawn anything except the boa constrictor from the outside and the inside since I was six. I shall try to make my portraits as true to life as possible. But I am

not at all sure of success.

One drawing goes along all right, and another has no resemblance to its subject. I make some errors, too, in the little prince's height: in one place he is too tall and in another too short. And I feel some doubts about the color of his costume. So I try my best.

I shall make mistakes about the details, also. But you must understand that is not my will. My friend never explained anything to me. He thought, perhaps, that I understood everything like him. But I, alas, cannot see the sheep inside the boxes. Perhaps I have become a grown-up. I have had to grow old.

Chapter 5

Each day, I learned about his planet little by little. I learned about his journey, the reasons why he left his planet. The information would come very slowly, as it might chance to fall from his thoughts. That was how, on the third day, I learned about the baobabs.

Once again, I learned about them because of the sheep. In a sudden, as if he was seized by doubt, the little prince asked me:

"It's true, isn't it, that sheep eat bushes?"

"Yes. That is true."

"Oh! I am glad."

baobab [`beəbæb] ***n.*** 猴麵包樹
bushe [bʊʃ] ***n.*** 灌木

I didn't understand why it was so important that the sheep ate bushes. But then the little prince asked:

"Does that mean that sheep also eat baobabs?"

I told him that baobabs were not bushes – they were trees as tall as castles. Even if he had many elephants, they would not be able to eat one single baobab.

The idea of so many elephants made the little prince laugh:

"We would have to put them on top of the other."

Then he made a wise comment:

"Before the baobabs grow so big, they start out by being little."

"That's true. But why do you want your sheep to eat the young baobabs?"

He said, "Oh, come on!" as if he was talking about something so obvious. But I had to listen carefully to understand what he said.

On the little prince's planet, as on all planets, there were good plants and bad plants. Good plants came from good seeds and bad plants came from bad seeds. They sleep in the ground until they decided to wake up and start growing, shyly at first as an innocent branch shooting up through the ground toward the sun. If it is only a sprout of radish or the sprig of a rose-bush, one would let it grow wherever it might wish. But when it is a bad plant, one must destroy it as soon as possible, the very first instant that one recognizes it.

* *

shoot up [ʃut ʌp] 生長

* *

There were some terrible seeds on the planet, the home of the little prince; and these were the seeds of the baobab. The soil of that planet was infested with them. If you fail to pull up a young baobab, it will spread over the entire planet. It will take over the whole planet. Its roots will tear through the planet. And if the planet is very small, and if there are too many baobabs, the baobabs will completely destroy the planet.

"It is a question of discipline," the little prince said to me later on.

"Each morning, I must take care of my planet. I have to pull up the little baobabs as soon as I can tell them apart from the young rose plants, since they are so alike. It is very tedious work," the little prince added, "but very easy."

And one day he said to me, "You should make a beautiful drawing, so that the children can see exactly how all this is."

* *

take over [tek `ovɚ] 接管
pull up [pʊl ʌp] 拔

* *

The Baobabs

"If they travel someday," he told me, "that would help them. Sometimes, there is no harm in putting off a piece of work until another day. But if it's a matter of baobabs, that always bring trouble. I knew a planet where a lazy man lived. He ignored three little bushes and..."

Therefore I drew this picture, as the little prince described it. In general, I do not like to tell people what they should do, but the danger of baobabs is not widely known. So this time, I will make an exception and say to you, "Children! Watch out for the baobabs!"

I have worked very hard on this picture. I hope it will teach my friends about the danger of the baobabs. The lesson I want to teach is meaningful even though it cost me a lot of trouble.

Perhaps you may ask "Why are there no other drawings in this book as magnificent and impressive as this drawing of the baobabs?"

The answer is simple: I tried my best. But with the others, I did not make it. When I drew the baobabs, I was carried beyond myself by the inspiring force of urgent necessity.

chapter 6

Oh! Little prince, bit by bit I came to understand the sadness of your little life. You never had much pleasure, except enjoying the beauty of sunsets. I learned this on the fourth morning when you said to me:

"I am very fond of sunsets. Come, let us go look at a sunset now."

"But we have to wait…"

"Wait? For what?"

"For the sunset. We must wait until it is time."

You looked very surprised at first, and then you

---

sadness [`sædnɪs] ***n.*** 悲傷
pleasure [`plɛʒɚ] ***n.*** 高興
except [ɪk`sɛpt] ***prep.*** 除……之外

laughed to yourself. And you said:

"For a moment, I thought I was still at home!"

As everyone knows, when it is noon in the United States, the sun is setting over France. If you could fly to France in one minute, you could go straight into the sunset, right from noon. Sadly, France is too far away. But, on your tiny planet, all you have to do is move your chair a few steps and you can watch the sunset whenever you like.

"One day," you said to me, "I saw the sunset forty-four times!"

And a little later you added:

"You know… one loves the sunset, when one is so sad..."

"Were you so sad, then?" I asked, "on the day of the forty-four sunsets?"

✶✶✶✶✶✶✶✶✶✶✶✶✶✶✶✶✶✶✶✶✶✶✶✶✶✶✶✶✶✶✶✶✶✶✶✶✶

sadly [ˋsædlɪ] ***adv.*** 可惜
far away [fɑr əˋwe] 遠處，（離……）很遠

✶✶✶✶✶✶✶✶✶✶✶✶✶✶✶✶✶✶✶✶✶✶✶✶✶✶✶✶✶✶✶✶✶✶✶✶✶

But the little prince did not answer me.

chapter 7

On the fifth day, I learned another secret of the little prince's life, thanks to the sheep. He suddenly asked me a question. It seemed that he had thought about this question for a long time:

"If a sheep eats bushes, will it eat flowers, too?"

"A sheep eats everything it comes across."

"Even flowers with thorns?"

"Yes. Even flowers with thorns."

"Then, why do they even have thorns?"

★★★★★★★★★★★★★★★★★★

secret [ˋsikrɪt] ***n.*** 祕密
thorn [θɔrn] ***n.*** 刺

★★★★★★★★★★★★★★★★★★

I didn't know. I was very busy trying to unscrew a bolt that had got stuck in my engine. I was quite worried, for it was becoming clear to me that the breakdown of my plane was extremely serious. And I did not have much drinking water left.

"So, why do they even have thorns?" The little prince never stopped asking a question once he had started. I was angry at the bolt. And I answered with the first thing that came into my head:

"The thorns are of no use at all. Flowers have thorns because they are mean!"

"Oh!"

There's a moment of silence, then he said angrily:

"I don't believe you! Flowers are weak. They are innocent and beautiful. They are just trying to protect themselves. They believe that the thorns keep them safe…"

* *

mean [min] ***adj.*** 卑鄙的
innocent [ˋɪnəsnt] ***adj.*** 無害的

* *

I did not answer. I was not listening. I was thinking about how to remove the bolt stuck in the engine. Then the little prince said to me:

"And you believe that flowers…"

"No! No! I don't believe anything! I answered you with the first thing that came into my head. I'm busy with something important right now!"

He stared at me, shocked, and cried:

"Something important!"

He looked at me as I was holding a hammer in my hand, and my fingers were dirty with black grease, bending down over an object which seemed to him extremely ugly ...

"You talk just like a grown-up!"

That made me feel bad. But he continued:

"You don't understand anything!"

He was really quite angry. He shook his golden-haired head:

"I know a planet where there is red-faced man. He has never smelled a flower. He has never looked at a star. He has never loved anyone. He has never done anything but add up numbers. Just like you, he says all day long, 'I'm busy with something important!' And that makes him swell up with pride. But he isn't a man… he's a mushroom!"

"A what?"

"A mushroom!"

The little prince was mad as hell:

"For millions of years, flowers have been growing thorns. And yet, for millions of years, sheep have been eating flowers. How can you say that it isn't important to try to understand why flowers keep growing thorns which can't stop the sheep from eating them? How can you say that the warfare between the sheep and the flowers doesn't matter? Isn't it more important than a fat red-faced man's math? I know one flower that is

unique to the world, which grows nowhere but on my planet, but one little sheep can destroy that flower in one single bite some morning, without even noticing what he is doing -- Oh! You think that is not important?" his face turned from white to red as he continued:

"If one loves a flower, and even it is the only blossom that grows in all the millions and millions of stars, that is enough to make him happy just to look at the stars. He can say to himself: 'My flower is somewhere out there…' But if the sheep eats the flower, then all his stars will be darkened in one moment. And you think that is not important!"

The little prince could not speak anymore. He cried and cried. The night had come. I stopped everything I had been doing. I didn't care about my plane, my hunger, or even the possibility of dying. On one star, one planet, my planet, the Earth, there was a sad little prince! I took him in my arms and rocked him. I told him: "The flower you love is not in danger... I will draw a muzzle for your sheep to stop it from eating your

* *

hunger [ˋhʌŋgɚ] ***n.*** 飢餓

* *

flower... I will draw railings to protect your flower… I will..." I did not know what to say. I felt helpless. I did not know how could I reach him…

It is such a secret place, the land of tears.

✶ ✶

helpless [ˋhɛlplɪs] ***adj.*** **無助的**

✶ ✶

chapter 8

I soon learned more about this flower. On the little prince's planet the flowers had always been very simple. They had only one ring of petals and took up very little room. They would appear one morning, and by night they would disappear. But one day, from a seed blown from no one knew where, a new flower had come up. The little prince cautiously observed the growing sprout which looked different from all the other small sprout on his planet. It might be a new kind of baobab.

Then this foreign plant started to blossom. The little prince observed the foreign flower as a large bud appeared, and he felt that this flower would become

* *

petal [`pɛtl̩] *n.* 花瓣
cautiously [`kɔʃəslɪ] *adj.* 小心地，謹慎地

* *

something special. However, the flower was not ready to reveal herself. In the protection of her green room, she continued the process of becoming beautiful by carefully choosing her colors and meticulously arranging her petals. She did not want to show herself like the wrinkled poppies. She only wanted to show her most beautiful self. Oh yes, she was quite vain! Her preparations for beauty lasted for days. Finally, one morning, just at sunrise, she revealed herself.

* *

vain [ven] ***adj.*** 炫耀的

preparation [ˌprɛpəˋreʃən] ***n.*** 準備

* *

After all the careful preparations, she said:

"Oh! I am not quite awake... You must excuse me...I am not ready to be seen..."

But the little prince could not stop admiring her:

"How beautiful you are!"

"I am, aren't I?" the flowser replied sweetly.

"And I was born just at the moment of sunrise..."

The little prince knew that she was rather vain, but she was so lovely and delicate! "I believe that it is time for breakfast," she told him. "If you would be so kind..."

And the little prince, feeling embarrassed, filled a sprinkling-can with fresh water and gave the flower her breakfast.

Soon she began to torture him with her vanity. One

* *

embarrassed [ɪm`bærəst] ***adj.*** 不好意思的

* *

day, for example, as they talked about her four thorns, she said to the little prince:

"Let the tigers come. I'm not afraid of their claws!"

"There are no tigers on my planet," the little prince pointed out. "And, anyway, tigers do not eat bushes."

"I am not a bush," the flower sweetly replied.

"I am sorry…"

"I'm not afraid of tigers. However, wind is not good for my health. Do you have a screen?"

"Wind is bad for her health… that is too bad," the little prince thought. "This flower is rather complicated…"

✶✶✶✶✶✶✶✶✶✶✶✶✶✶✶✶✶✶✶✶✶✶✶✶✶✶✶✶✶✶✶

screen [skrin] ***n.*** 屏風

✶✶✶✶✶✶✶✶✶✶✶✶✶✶✶✶✶✶✶✶✶✶✶✶✶✶✶✶✶✶✶

"Please put me under a glass globe to keep me warm every night. It is very cold here. In the place I came from…"

But she stopped herself. She had arrived in the form of a seed. She had never been to any other planets. She felt embarrassed for being caught telling such a lie. Then she coughed two or three times:

"Do you have a screen?"

"I was about to go and find it, but you were speaking to me!"

✶✶✶✶✶✶✶✶✶✶✶✶✶✶✶✶✶✶✶✶✶✶✶✶✶✶✶✶✶✶✶✶

globe [glob] ***n.*** 球狀物

✶✶✶✶✶✶✶✶✶✶✶✶✶✶✶✶✶✶✶✶✶✶✶✶✶✶✶✶✶✶✶✶

Then she coughed again to make him feel bad.

And that is how the little prince began to doubt the flower he loved. He had taken what she said seriously, and now he was unhappy.

“I should not have listened to her,” He told me one day, “You should never listen to what flowers say. You should only look at them and smell them. Mine perfumed my planet, but I didn’t realize back then. Her comments about the tiger claws should have touched me instead of irritated me…”

He continued:

“I never really understood her! I should have judged her by her deeds and not by her words. She made my world become beautiful. I should never have left! I should have seen the tenderness beneath her foolish little games. Flowers are so complicated! Sadly, I was too young to know how to love her.”

chapter 9

I believe that some wild birds helped the little prince leave his planet. On the morning of the day he left, he put his planet in good order. He carefully cleaned the active volcanoes.

There were two active volcanoes. They were quite useful for cooking his breakfast in the mornings. He also had an extinct volcano. But, as he said, "You never know!" So he cleaned the extinct volcano, too. As long as they were clean, the volcanoes burned gently and steadily without eruptions. Volcano eruptions are like fires in a chimney. On Earth, we are obviously way too small to clean out our volcanoes, which is why they can create so much disaster.

The little prince also pulled up the latest baobab shoots. He felt rather sad because he believed that he

* *

volcano [val`keno] *n.* 火山

* *

would never want to return. When he prepared to put his flower under her glass globe after watering it for the very last time, he wanted to cry.

"Goodbye," he said to the flower.

But she did not answer.

"Goodbye," he said again.

The flower coughed. But she was not coughing because having a cold.

"I have been a fool," she finally said. "I am sorry for the way I acted. Please try to be happy."

The little prince was surprised that she was not angry with him. He stood there holding the glass globe. He did not know what to do. He did not understand her

gentle tenderness.

"I love you," the flower told him. "But you didn't know that because of the way I acted. But none of this is important now. And you were just as foolish as I was. Try to be happy… don't worry about the glass globe. I don't want it anymore."

"But the cold night air…"

"I am not that weak… the cool night air will be good for me. I am a flower."

"But the wild animals…"

"If I want to meet butterflies, I must put up with two or three caterpillars. I've heard that butterflies are very beautiful. Besides, who else will visit me? You will be far away. And I am not afraid of wild animals. I have my claws."

* *

foolish [ˋfulɪʃ] ***adj.*** 傻的
weak [wik] ***adj.*** 虛弱的
put up with [pʊt ʌp wɪð] 忍受
caterpillar [ˋkætɚˌpɪlɚ] ***n.*** 毛蟲

* *

And she innocently showed her four thorns.

Then she added:

"Don't just stand around. You have decided to go. Then go."

She did not want him to see her crying. She was a very proud flower…

* *

stand around [stænd ə`raʊnd] 坐著不做事，懶散地消磨時間

* *

Chapter 10

The little prince found himself near asteroids 325, 326, 327, 328, 329, and 330. He decided to visit each of them to learn more about the world.

On the first asteroid, there lived a king. The king sat on a simple but beautiful throne, wearing a wonderful purple robe.

"Aha! Here is a subject!" cried the king, when he saw the little prince.

And the little prince asked himself:

"How does he know who I am? He has never seen me before."

throne [θron] ***n.*** 王座
robe [rob] ***n.*** 長袍
subject [ˋsʌbdʒɪkt] ***n.*** 臣民

He did not know that, for kings, the world is very simple. All men are their subjects.

"Come to me so that I can see you better," said the king. He was very proud to finally have a subject.

The little prince looked for a place to sit down. But the planet was covered by the king's robe, so he remained standing. And because he was tired, he yawned.

The King told him:

"Yawning in front of a king is not allowed. I forbid you to yawn."

"I could not help yawning," answered the little prince, feeling bad. "I have traveled a long way, and I have not slept…"

"Then," said the king, "I demand that you yawn. I have not seen anyone yawn for years. Yawns interest me. Go on! Yawn again. That is an order."

* *

yawn [jɔn] *v.* 打呵欠

* *

"Now I feel embarrassed… I can't yawn anymore," the little prince said, turning red in the face.

"Hum! Hum!" said the king. "Well then, I… I order you to yawn sometimes and to…"

He stopped speaking, and seemed angry.

Above all, the king wanted to be sure that his power is respected. He did not allow anybody to disobey him. But, because he was very sensible, his orders were always reasonable.

"If I ordered my general to change himself into a

bird, and if the general did not obey, that would not be his fault. That would be my fault."

"May I sit down?" the little prince asked.

"I order you to sit down," the king replied. He carefully moved his purple robe.

But the little prince was wondering… The planet was very small. What did the king rule over?

"Sire," he said, "please excuse me for asking you this…"

"I order you to ask me," the king quickly said.

"Sire…what exactly do you rule over?"

"Everything," answered the king.

"Over everything?"

* *

rule over [rul`ovɚ] *v.* 統治
Sire [saɪr] *n.* 陛下

* *

The king pointed to his planet, the other planets, and all the stars.

"Over all that?" asked the little prince.

"Over all that…" replied the king.

Because the king not only ruled his own planet, but everything else as well. "And do the stars follow your orders?"

"Of course," the king told him. "They obey me completely. I would not allow them to disobey me."

Such great power shocked the little prince. If he had such power himself, he could have watched, not just forty-four, but seventy-two or even one hundred, or even two hundred sunsets in a single day, without ever having to move his chair! Since he felt rather sad thinking of his own little planet, which he had left behind, he decided to ask the king for something:

"I would like to see a sunset… Would you do me that kindness? Please ask the sun to set…"

"If I ordered a general to fly from one flower to another like a butterfly, or to write a novel, or to turn into a bird, and the general did not follow my orders, who would be wrong?"

"You would be wrong," the little prince answered firmly.

"Exactly. As king, I must order each subject to do things he can do," said the king. "My power comes from sensible rules. If I ordered my subjects to throw themselves into the sea, they would rise against my rule. I have the right to rule them because my orders make sense."

"What about my sunset?" asked the little prince again. He never forgot a question once he had asked.

"You shall have your sunset. I order it. But I shall wait until the time is right."

"When will the time be right?" asked the little prince.

* *

make sense [mek sɛns] 頗具意義

* *

"Ahem! Ahem!" the king replied. He looked at a large calendar. "Ahem! Ahem! That will be around… around… that will be this evening around seven-forty! And you will see how well my orders are followed."

The little prince yawned. He wished that he could have his sunset; he was feeling bored, as well.

"There is nothing else for me to do here," he said to the king. "I will be on my way!"

"Do not leave," replied the king. He was so proud to have a subject. "Do not leave… I will let you be my minister!"

"Minister of what?"

"Of…of justice!"

"But there is nobody here to be judged!"

* *

Ahem [ə`hɛm] ***int.*** 嗯哼！
minister [`mɪnɪstɚ] ***n.*** 大臣
justice [`dʒʌstɪs] ***n.*** 正義
judge [dʒʌdʒ] ***v.*** 審判

* *

"You never know," said the king. "I have not seen all of my kingdom yet. I am very old and I have no way to travel. Walking makes me tired."

"Oh! But I've already seen it!" said the little prince. He looked at the other side of the planet one more time. "There is no one living there, either."

"Then you shall judge yourself," said the king. "That is the most difficult job of all. Judging yourself is much harder than judging another person. If you can judge yourself, you will be a very wise man."

"I can judge myself anywhere, though," said the little prince. "I do not need to live here to do that."

"Ahem! Ahem!" said the king. "I believe that an old rat lives somewhere on my planet. I can hear him at night. You will judge this old rat. You will condemn him to death from time to time, but you will then pardon him each time. We must not be wasteful as he is the only rat."

✶✶✶✶✶✶✶✶✶✶✶✶✶✶✶✶✶✶✶✶✶✶✶✶✶✶✶✶✶✶✶✶

kingdom [ˋkɪŋdəm] ***n.*** 王國

✶✶✶✶✶✶✶✶✶✶✶✶✶✶✶✶✶✶✶✶✶✶✶✶✶✶✶✶✶✶✶✶

"I don't like the idea of condemning something to death," the little prince said. "I think that I should go."

"No," said the king.

The little prince did not want to enrage the old king:

"If Your Majesty wants to be obeyed, Your Majesty should give me a reasonable order. For example, you should order me to leave in less than one minute. I think that it is time to…"

The king did not answer. The little prince waited for a moment. Then, with a sigh, he left the king's planet.

"I will let you be my ambassador," the king shouted in haste.

He spoke with great power.

"Grown-ups are rather strange," the little prince said to himself as he left.

Chapter 11

One the second planet, there lived a very vain man. "Aha! Here comes an admirer!" he shouted, as soon as he saw the little prince.

For vain people, everyone is their admirer.

"Good morning," said the little prince. "You are wearing a strange hat."

"This hat is made for greeting new people," the vain man told him. "Sadly, no one ever comes here."

"Really?" said the little prince. He did not understand.

"Clap your hands together," the vain man said.

The little prince clapped his hands. The vain man raised his hat in a salute.

"This is more fun than my visit to the king," the little prince said to himself. And he clapped his hands some more. The vain man tipped his hat again.

After five minutes of clapping, the little prince was bored.

"What should I do to make the hat come down from your head?" he asked.

The vain man did not hear him. Vain people never listen to anything except admiration.

"Do you really admire me a lot?" he asked the little prince.

* *

clap [klæp] *v.* 鼓掌
raise [rez] *v.* 舉起
tip [tɪp] *v.* 脫帽致意

* *

"What does 'admire' mean?" the little prince said.

"To admire me means that you consider me the most beautiful, the best-dressed, the richest, and the most intelligent person on this planet."

"But you are the only person on this planet!"

"Please admire me anyway!"

"I admire you," said the little prince, who did not understand, "But why does this matter so much to you?"

And then the little prince left the planet.

"Grown-ups are really very strange," the little prince said to himself as he continued on his way.

* *

consider [kən`sɪdɚ] ***v.*** 認為
strange [strendʒ] ***adj.*** 奇怪的

* *

Chapter 12

On the next planet, there lived a drunkard. The little prince's visit to this planet was very short, but it made him extremely sad.

"What do you do here?" he asked the drunkard. The drunkard had many bottles in front of him. Some of the bottles were empty, and some of them were full.

"I drink," answered the drunkard, with an lugubrious voice.

extremely [ɪk`strimlɪ] ***adv.*** 非常
drunkard [`drʌŋkɚd] ***n.*** 醉漢
empty [`ɛmptɪ] ***adj.*** 空的

"Why do you drink?" the little prince asked him.

"So I can forget," said the drunkard.

"Forget what?" asked the little prince, who already felt sad for him.

"Forget how terrible I feel," the drunkard told him, sinking in his seat.

"What do you feel terrible about?" the little prince asked. He wanted to help him.

"Terrible about drinking!" answered the drunkard. He said no more.

So the little prince left. He did not understand what the drunkard said.

"Grown-ups are really quite, quite strange," he said to himself.

forget [fɚˋgɛt] ***v.*** 忘記
terrible [ˋtɛrəbl̩] ***adj.*** 可怕的
quite [kwaɪt] ***adv.*** 完全

Chapter 13

On the fourth planet, there lived a businessman. This man was so busy that he was not even aware of the little prince's arrival.

"Hello," the little prince said. "Your cigarette has gone out."

"Three plus two makes five. Five plus seven makes twelve. Twelve plus three makes fifteen. Hello. Fifteen plus seven makes twenty-two. Twenty-two plus six makes twenty-eight. I don't have time to light it again. Twenty-six plus five make thirty-one. Whew! Then that makes five-hundred-and-one million, six-hundred-and-twenty-two thousand, seven hundred and thirty-one."

"Five hundred million of what?" asked the little prince.

"What? You're still here? Five-hundred-and-one million... I don't remember... I have so much to do! I am an important man! I don't have time for silly games! Two plus five makes seven…"

"Five-hundred-and-one million of what?" asked the little prince again. He never stopped asking a question

✶✶✶✶✶✶✶✶✶✶✶✶✶✶✶✶✶✶✶✶✶✶✶✶✶✶✶✶✶✶✶

hundred [ˋhʌndrəd] ***n.*** 一百
million [ˋmɪljən] ***n.*** 百萬
thousand [ˋθaʊznd] ***n.*** 一千

✶✶✶✶✶✶✶✶✶✶✶✶✶✶✶✶✶✶✶✶✶✶✶✶✶✶✶✶✶✶✶

once he had asked it.

The businessman looked up. He said:

"For fifty-four years I have lived on this planet, I have been forced to stop only three times. The first time was twenty-two years ago when a bug dropped from who knows where. It made the most awful noise, and I made four mistakes in my math.

"The second time was eleven years ago when I became ill. I do not get enough exercise. I have no time to waste. I am an important man. The third time… is right now! As I was saying, five-hundred-and-one million…"

"Millions of what?"

The businessman realized that the little prince would not stop his question. He answered:

"Millions of those little objects you sometimes see in

✶✶✶✶✶✶✶✶✶✶✶✶✶✶✶✶✶✶✶✶✶✶✶✶✶✶✶✶✶✶✶✶

math [mæθ] ***n.*** 數學

✶✶✶✶✶✶✶✶✶✶✶✶✶✶✶✶✶✶✶✶✶✶✶✶✶✶✶✶✶✶✶✶

the sky."

"Flies?"

"No, no. The little objects that shine."

"Bees?"

"No. The golden objects that make lazy people dream. However, I am an important man! I don't have time for sitting around and dreaming."

"Oh! You mean the stars?" said the little prince.

"Yes, That's right. The Stars"

"And what do you do with five-hundred million of stars?"

"Five-hundred-and-one million, six-hundred-and-twenty-two thousand, seven hundred and thirty-one stars. I am an important man. I sum them accurately."

✶✶✶✶✶✶✶✶✶✶✶✶✶✶✶✶✶✶✶✶✶✶✶✶✶✶✶✶✶✶✶✶✶

object [`ɑbdʒɪkt] ***n.*** 物體

✶✶✶✶✶✶✶✶✶✶✶✶✶✶✶✶✶✶✶✶✶✶✶✶✶✶✶✶✶✶✶✶✶

"And what do you do with these stars?"

"What do I do with them?"

"Yes."

"Nothing. I own them."

"You own the stars?"

"Yes."

"But I have already met a king who…"

"Kings do not own things. They rule over things. It's very different," the businessman told him.

"Why does it matter that you own the stars?"

"It makes me rich."

"Why does it matter that you are rich?"

✶✶✶✶✶✶✶✶✶✶✶✶✶✶✶✶✶✶✶✶✶✶✶✶✶✶✶✶✶✶✶✶

own [on] ***v.*** 擁有

✶✶✶✶✶✶✶✶✶✶✶✶✶✶✶✶✶✶✶✶✶✶✶✶✶✶✶✶✶✶✶✶

"Being rich lets me buy other stars, if anyone finds some."

"This man thinks in the same way as the drunkard," the little prince said to himself. However, he asked a few more questions:

"How can you own the stars?"

"Who else owns them?" the businessman answered angrily.

"I don't know. Nobody owns them."

"Well then, they are mine because I was the first person to think of owning them."

"Is that enough?"

"Of course it is. When you find a diamond that no one owns, it is yours. When you find an island that no one owns, it is yours. When you are the first person to have the idea, you own it. So now, I own the stars because nobody else ever thought of owning them."

"That makes sense," said the little prince. "And what do you do with them?"

"I count them and recount them," said the businessman. "It is a difficult work, but I am an important man!"

The little prince did not finish asking questions.

"If I own a scarf, I can put it around my neck and take it with me. If I own a flower, I can pick it up and take it with me, but you cannot take the stars with you!"

"No, but I can put them in the bank," said the businessman.

"What does that mean?"

"That means I write down the number of the stars I own on a piece of paper, and then I put the paper in a drawer and lock it up."

"That's all?"

"That's enough!"

"How funny," thought the little prince.

"It's an interesting idea, but it does not make much sense." The little prince thought very differently about important matters. He said to the businessman:

"I own a flower which I water every day. I own three volcanoes, which I clean once a week, even the extinct one. I am useful to my flower and to my volcanoes, but you are not useful to the stars."

The businessman opened his mouth but could not think of anything to say. So the little prince left the planet.

"Grown-ups are really very strange," he said to himself as he went on his way.

chapter 14

The fifth planet was very strange. It was the smallest of all. There was just enough space for a streetlamp and a lamplighter. The little prince could not understand why there was a streetlamp and a lamplighter on a planet without houses or other people. However, he said to himself:

"Maybe the presence of this lamplighter is silly. However, he is less silly than the king, the vain man, the businessman, and the drunkard. At least the lamplighter's job means something. When he lights his lamp, it's as if he's bringing one more star or flower to life. When he puts out his lamp, it's as if he is putting a star or a flower to sleep. It is a rather beautiful job and it is beautiful because it is useful."

* *

streetlamp [ˋstrit͵læmp] ***n.*** 街燈
lamplighter [ˋlæmp͵laɪtɚ] ***n.***（舊時）點燃街燈的燈伕
silly [ˋsɪlɪ] ***adj.*** 愚蠢的

* *

Once the little prince arrived on the planet, he greeted the lamplighter:

"Hello. Why did you put out your streetlamp?"

"Those are the orders," answered the lamplighter. "Good morning."

"What are the orders?"

"To put out the lamp. Good evening." And he lit the streetlight again.

"But why did you just light the lamp again?" asked the little prince.

"Those are the orders," the lamplighter told him.

"I don't understand," said the little prince.

"There is nothing to understand," answered the lamplighter. "Orders are orders. Good morning." And

* *

put out [pʊt aʊt] 撲滅
order [ˋɔrdɚ] ***n.*** 規則

* *

he put out the lamp.

Then he wiped his face with a handkerchief.

"I have a terrible job. It used to make sense. I put out the lamp in the mornings and then lighted it at night. I had the rest of the day to relax and the rest of the night to sleep..."

"And since then the orders have changed?"

"The orders have not changed," said the lamplighter. "That is the problem! Each year this planet turns more and more quickly, but the orders have not changed!"

"So what does that mean?" asked the little prince.

"Now the planet completes a rotation once every minute, and I have no time to rest. I light and put out the lamp once every minute!"

"How funny! The day here on your planet lasts for just one minute!"

rest [rɛst] ***n.*** 剩餘

“It’s not funny at all,” said the lamplighter. “We have already been talking for a whole month.”

“A month?”

"Yes. Thirty minutes! Thirty days! Good evening." And he lit the streetlamp again.

The little prince admired this lamplighter who was so faithful to his orders. He remembered the sunsets on his own planet, and how he tried to watch them by moving his chair. He wanted to help the lamplighter. He said:

"I know how you can rest when you need to..."

"I always need a rest," said the lamplighter.

It is possible to follow orders and still be lazy at the same time.

The little prince continued:

"Your planet is so small that you can walk around it in three steps. If you walk slowly, you will always be in the sunshine. So when you want to rest, you can walk... and the day will last as long as you like."

"That will not help me much," said the lamplighter. "What I really want to do is sleep."

"Then there is nothing else you can do," said the little prince.

"I know," agreed the lamplighter. "Good morning." And he put out the lamp.

As he continued his travels, the little prince said to himself:

"That lamplighter would be looked down on by everyone else I have met: the king, the vain man, the drunkard, and the businessman. However, he is the only one who does not seem silly to me. Maybe that is because he is the only one who is thinking of something other than himself."

The little prince sighed and said to himself:

"He is the only one who could have been my friend but his planet is really too small. There is no space for two…"

The little prince also wished that he could stay on the little planet because it had one thousand four hundred and forty sunsets every twenty-four hours!

Chapter 15

The sixth planet was ten times bigger than the last one. There lived an old man who wrote very large books.

"Well! Here is an explorer!" cried the old man when he saw the little prince.

The little prince was tired and sat down on the man's table. He had already traveled so far!

"Where do you come from?" the old man asked.

"What is this large book? What are you doing here?" asked the little prince.

"I am a geographer," said the old man.

explorer [ɪk`splorɚ] ***n.*** 探險家
geographer [dʒɪ`ɑgrəfɚ] ***n.*** 地理學家

"What is a geographer?"

"A geographer is a person who knows where all the oceans, rivers, cities, mountains, and deserts are."

"That is very interesting," said the little prince. "At last, this is a real job!" And he looked around at the geographer's planet. He had never seen such a large and beautiful planet.

"Your planet is very beautiful. Are there many oceans?"

"I do not know," answered the geographer.

"Oh," the little prince was disappointed. "Are there mountains?"

"I do not know," said the geographer.

"And cities and rivers and deserts?"

"I do not know that, either," said the geographer.

interesting [ˋɪntərɪstɪŋ] ***adj.*** **有趣的**

"But you are a geographer!"

"That is correct," said the geographer. "But I am not an explorer. There are no explorers here. It is not a geographer's job to look for cities or rivers or mountains or oceans or deserts. A geographer is too important to do that. A geographer never leaves his desk but I talk to explorers and I write down what they have seen. If I am interested in what an explorer says, then I will find out whether the explorer is an honest person or not."

"Why?"

"Because an explorer who lies would create terrible problems with geography books. An explorer who drank too much would create problems, as well."

"Why?" asked the little prince.

"Because drunkards see double and then I would note down two mountains where there was only one."

"I know one who would be a bad explorer," said the little prince.

"That is possible. And so once I know that an explorer is honest, I must study his discovery."

"Do you go and see it?"

"No. That would be difficult. But the explorer must prove to me that his discovery is real. If the explorer has discovered a large mountain, then I demand that he show me some large rocks."

✶✶✶✶✶✶✶✶✶✶✶✶✶✶✶✶✶✶✶✶✶✶✶✶✶✶✶✶✶✶✶✶

prove [pruv] *v.* 證明

✶✶✶✶✶✶✶✶✶✶✶✶✶✶✶✶✶✶✶✶✶✶✶✶✶✶✶✶✶✶✶✶

The geographer suddenly became excited.

He cried:

"But you come from far away! You are an explorer! You must tell me about your planet!"

The geographer opened his book and took out his pencil. He always wrote with a pencil first. He waited until the explorer had proved his discovery before he wrote with a pen.

"Well?" said the geographer.

"Oh, my home is not very interesting," said the little prince.

"It is very small. I have three volcanoes. Two are active, and one is asleep. But you will never know."

"You will never know," said the geographer.

"I also have a flower."

* *

excited [ɪkˋsaɪtɪd] ***adj.*** 興奮的

* *

"I do not write about flowers," said the geographer.

"Why not? They are so beautiful!"

"Because flowers are ephemeral."

"What do you mean by 'ephemeral'?"

"Geography books are the most important of all books," said the geographer. "The information in the books never changes. It is very rare for a mountain to move around. It is very rare for an ocean to become dry. Geographers only write about things that never change."

"But a sleeping volcano can wake up again," said the little prince. "What do you mean by 'ephemeral'?"

"Whether a volcano is asleep or active does not matter to geographers. What matters to us is the mountain. It does not change."

* *

ephemeral [ɪˋfɛmərəl] ***n.*** 短暫的事物

* *

"But what does 'ephemeral' mean?" repeated the little prince. He never stopped asking a question once he had started asking it.

"It means 'something that will not last.'"

"My flower will not last?"

"That's right."

"My flower is ephemeral," the little prince said to himself. "She only has four thorns to protect herself against the world! And I left her all alone."

Suddenly he wished that he had not left but he tried to be brave:

"What planet should I visit?" he asked the geographer.

"The planet Earth," the geographer answered. "It is thought to be a fine planet."

And the little prince left, thinking of his flower.

Chapter 16

And so the seventh planet that the little prince visited was the Earth.

The planet Earth is a rather interesting planet! There are one hundred eleven kings, seven thousand geographers, nine-hundred thousand businessmen, seven-and-a-half million drunkards, and three-hundred-eleven million vain people. In all, there are about two billion grown-ups.

To give you a sense of the Earth's size, I will tell you that, before the invention of electricity, there were about four-hundred-and-sixty-two thousand, five hundred and eleven lamplighters in six continents.

rather [`ræðɚ] *adv.* 相當
billion [`bɪljən] *n.* 十億
invention [ɪn`vɛnʃən] *n.* 發明

Seen from high above in the sky, they made the Earth a beautiful sight. These lamplighters worked together like dancers on a great stage. To start, the lamplighters in New Zealand and Australia would light their lamps before going to bed. The lamplighters in China and Siberia lit their lamps next. Then the lamplighters of Russia and India. Then those of Africa and of Europe. Then the lamplighters of South America, and finally those of North America. And these lamplighters never lit their lamps in the wrong order. Their dance was perfect. It was beautiful to see.

The simplest jobs were the lamplighters at the North Pole and the South Pole: they only worked twice each year.

* *

lit [lɪt] ***v.*** 點（火）；點燃
the North Pole [ðə nɔrθ pol] ***n.*** 北極
the South Pole [ðə saʊθ pol] ***n.*** 南極

* *

Chapter 17

When I want to be funny, sometimes I find myself telling a little lie. I have not been completely truthful in writing about lamplighters. I am in danger of confusing people who do not know our planet well. In fact, people occupy very little space on the Earth. If the two billion people of Earth lived in one place together, they could easily fit in an area only twenty miles long and twenty miles wide. All the people on Earth could live together on the smallest island in the Pacific Ocean.

Of course, grown-ups will not believe this. They like to think that they occupy a lot of space. They believe they are big and important, like baobabs. Since they won't believe you, tell them to calculate the smallest area themselves. But do not waste your time worrying about them. There is no reason. Believe me.

lie [laɪ] ***n.*** 謊言
the Pacific Ocean [ðə pə`sɪfɪk `oʃən] ***n.*** 太平洋

Once he reached the Earth, the little prince was very surprised that he was all alone. He did not see anyone. He was afraid that he had come to the wrong planet. Then he saw something golden moving in the sand.

"Good evening," said the little prince.

"Good evening," said the snake.

"What planet is this?" asked the little prince.

"You are on the Earth, in Africa," the snake said.

"Oh! Then no one lives on the Earth?"

"This is the desert. No one lives in the desert. The Earth is very big," answered the snake.

The little prince sat down on a stone. He looked up at the sky.

"I wonder whether the stars shine so that one day

* *

snake [snek] ***n.*** 蛇

* *

everyone can find their own," he said. "Look at my planet. It is just above us… But how far away it is!"

"It is beautiful," said the snake. "Then why have you come here?"

"I have problems with a flower," said the little prince.

"Ah," said the snake.

Neither of them spoke.

"Where are the people?" the little prince finally asked. "I am lonely in the desert…"

"It is lonely among the people, too," said the snake.

The little prince looked at the snake for a long time.

"You are a strange-looking animal," he told the snake.

"You are long and thin like a finger…"

* *

lonely [ˋlonlɪ] ***adj.*** 孤獨的

* *

"But I am more powerful than the finger of a king," the snake said.

The little prince smiled:

"How can you be powerful…you do not even have feet… you cannot move easily."

"I can take you far, far away," said the snake, and wrapped itself around the little prince's ankle like a golden bracelet:

"Whomever I touch, I send back to the earth from where he came," the snake said. "But you are pure. You come from a star…"

The little prince said nothing.

"I feel sorry for you. You are so weak and alone on the Earth. Someday I may be able to help if you miss your planet too much. I can…"

"Oh! I understand," said the little prince. "But why do you always speak in riddles?"

"I solve all riddles," said the snake. And both were quiet.

✶✶✶✶✶✶✶✶✶✶✶✶✶✶✶✶✶✶✶✶✶✶✶✶✶✶✶✶✶✶✶✶✶

ankle [ˋæŋk!] ***n.*** 足踝
riddle [ˋrɪd!] ***n.*** 謎語

✶✶✶✶✶✶✶✶✶✶✶✶✶✶✶✶✶✶✶✶✶✶✶✶✶✶✶✶✶✶✶✶✶

chapter 18

The little prince crossed the desert. He met no one except a flower with only three petals.

"Hello," said the little prince.

"Hello," said the flower.

"Have you seen any people?" the little prince asked.

The flower had once seen some travelers pass by:

"People? I have seen some, I guess, about six or seven. I saw them years ago, but I do not know where they are. The wind blows them here and there. They do not have roots and that makes their lives quite difficult."

"Goodbye," said the little prince.

"Goodbye," said the flower.

✶✶✶✶✶✶✶✶✶✶✶✶✶✶✶✶✶✶✶✶✶✶✶✶✶✶✶✶✶✶✶✶

roots [rut] ***n.***（植物的）根
difficult [ˋdɪfəˏkəlt] ***adj.*** 困難的

✶✶✶✶✶✶✶✶✶✶✶✶✶✶✶✶✶✶✶✶✶✶✶✶✶✶✶✶✶✶✶✶

The little prince climbed a tall mountain. The only mountains he had ever known were his three volcanoes, which came up to his knees. He had used the extinct volcano as a footstool.

"I should be able to see the whole planet and all the people from such a tall mountain," he said to himself but all he could see were rocks and mountains.

"Hello," he called out.

"Hello…Hello…Hello… ," the echo answered.

"Who are you?" asked the little prince.

* *

climb [klaɪm] ***v.*** 攀登
whole [hol] ***adj.*** 全部的
echo [ˋɛko] ***n.*** 回聲

* *

"Who are you… Who are you… Who are you… ?" answered the echo.

"Be my friends. I am alone," he said.

"I am alone… I am alone… I am alone…" answered the echo.

"What a strange planet," the little prince thought. "It is dry and full of mountains and the people here are not very interesting. They repeat whatever one says to them. At home I had a flower: she was always the first to speak…"

alone [ə`lon] ***adj.*** 單獨的
thought [θɔt] ***n.*** 思考
whatever [hwɑt`ɛvɚ] ***pron.*** 不管什麼

chapter 20

After a long time, the little prince found a road. And all roads lead to the world of people.

"Hello," said the little prince. He was in a rose garden.

"Hello," said the roses.

The little prince looked at them. They were like his flower.

"Who are you?" he demanded, feeling shocked.

"We are roses," said the roses.

"Oh!" said the little prince.

And he felt very sad. His flower had told him that she was unique, the only one in the universe and here were five thousand flowers that looked just like her, in a single garden!

"If my flower saw this, she would be very unhappy," he said to himself. She would cough and pretend that she was dying in order to escape from being laughed at and I would have to pretend to take care of her. Otherwise, she might really let herself die to make me

✦✦✦✦✦✦✦✦✦✦✦✦✦✦✦✦✦✦✦✦✦✦✦✦✦✦✦✦✦✦✦✦

unique [juˋnik] ***adj.*** 獨一無二的
universe [ˋjunəˏvɝs] ***n.*** 宇宙
cough [kɔf] ***v.*** 咳嗽
pretend [prɪˋtɛnd] ***v.*** 假裝
otherwise [ˋʌðɚˏwaɪz] ***adv.*** 否則

✦✦✦✦✦✦✦✦✦✦✦✦✦✦✦✦✦✦✦✦✦✦✦✦✦✦✦✦✦✦✦✦

look bad."

Then he said to himself: "I thought I was rich. I thought I had a special flower, but in reality she is only an ordinary rose. As for my three volcanoes, they are very small and one of them is extinct. That doesn't make me a very great prince." The little prince laid down on the grass and he cried and cried.

ordinary [ˋɔrdn͵ɛrɪ] *adj.* 平凡的

Chapter 21

It was then that the fox appeared.
"Hello," said the fox.

"Hello," the little prince answered. Although he had turned around he did not see anyone.

"I am here," said a voice under the apple tree.

"Who are you?" said the little prince. "You are quite beautiful."

"I am a fox," said the fox.

"Come play with me," the little prince said. "I am so sad."

"I cannot play with you," answered the fox. "I am not tame."

* *

tame [tem] *adj.*（動物）經馴養的

* *

"Oh! Excuse me," said the little prince. After thinking for a while, he added, "What does 'tame' mean?"

"You are not from around here," said the fox. "What are you doing here?"

"I am looking for people," said the little prince. "What does 'tame' mean?"

"People have guns. They go hunting," said the fox. "It is very inconvenient. They also raise chickens. That is all they do. Are you looking for chickens?"

"No," said the little prince. "I am looking for friends. What does 'tame' mean?"

"It means something that too many people have forgotten," said the fox. "To tame means 'to create ties or form a bond.' Right now, to me, you are a little boy just like thousands of other little boys. I do not need you and you do not need me, either. For you, I am a fox just like thousands of other foxes. But if you tame me,

inconvenient [ˌɪnkənˋvinjənt] ***adj.*** 打擾的
bond [bɑnd] ***n.*** 聯結

we will need each other. For me, you will be unique in the world. You will be different from everyone else and I will be unique for you…"

"I think that I am beginning to understand," said the little prince. "There was once a flower… I think she tamed me…"

"It is possible," said the fox. "Many things are possible on the Earth."

"Oh! This did not happen on the Earth," said the little prince. The fox looked at him with interest:

"It happened on another planet?"

"Yes."

"Are there hunters on that planet?"

"No."

"How interesting! Are there chickens?"

"No."

"Nothing is perfect," the fox sighed.

He began to speak again. "My life is always the same. I hunt chickens, and people hunt me. All chickens seem the same, and all people seem the same; therefore, I get rather bored. But if you tame me, then my life will be filled with sunshine. I will run and hide when I hear the sound of other people's footsteps, but your footsteps will sound different. When I hear your footsteps, they will sound like music to me and I will come and greet you. And look! Do you see that field of wheat over there?

* *

footstep [ˋfʊtˏstɛp] ***n.*** 腳步
wheat [hwit] ***n.*** 小麥

* *

"Because I do not eat bread, what is not important to me. Wheat does not make me think of anything and that is sad! But you have golden hair. That will be so wonderful when you tame me! The golden wheat will make me think of you and I will love listening to the sounds of the wind in the wheat..."

Then the fox was quiet. He looked at the little prince for a long time.

At last he said, "Please... tame me!"

"I would like to very much," answered the little prince. "But I do not have much time. I have friends to make and many things to learn."

"We only learn the things that we have tamed," said the fox. "People today are too busy to truly know anything. They go to shops to buy things that have already been made. However, there are no shops for selling friends so people no longer have friends. If you want a friend, tame me!"

"What must I do?" asked the little prince.

"You must be very patient," the fox told him. "First you must sit in the grass, rather far away from me. I will watch you carefully. You will not say a word. All misunderstanding comes from talking, but each day you will be able to sit a little bit closer to me..."

On the next day the little prince returned.

"It would be better if you returned at the same time every day," said the fox. "If you always come at four o'clock in the afternoon, then I will be happy around three. The nearer it gets to four o'clock, the happier I will feel. At four, I will be so excited! I will know what happiness is! But if you come at a different time each day, I will not know when I should start to be happy... we must have a ritual."

"What is a ritual?" asked the little prince.

"That is something else that too many people have forgotten," said the fox. "A ritual is what makes one day different from another, or one hour different from

* *

patient [ˋpeʃənt] ***adj.*** 有耐心的
ritual [ˋrɪtʃʊəl] ***n.*** 儀式

* *

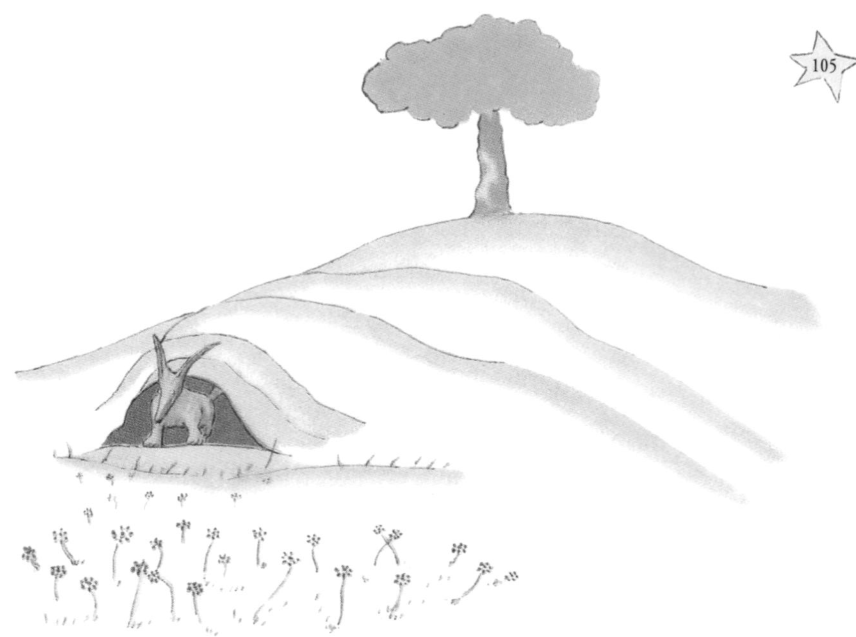

other hours. For example, my hunters have a ritual. Every Thursday they go dancing with the village girls. That is why every Thursday is a wonderful day! I can take walks all over. If the hunters danced any time they want, then every day would resemble the others, and I would never have a rest."

So the little prince tamed the fox. When it was about the time for the little prince to leave, the fox said:

"Oh! I will cry..."

* *

resemble [rɪˋzɛmb!] *v.* 像

* *

"That is your fault," answered the little prince. "I did not want to hurt you, but you asked me to tame you..."

"Of course," said the fox.

"But you will cry!"

"Of course."

"Then what do you get from this? Why did you do this? What is your reason?" asked the little prince.

"My reason lies in the golden color of the wheat," answered the fox.

Then he added:

"Go back and look at the roses. You will see that yours is unique. Then come here and say goodbye to me, and I will tell you a secret. It will be my gift to you."

The little prince went back and looked at the roses.

✶✶✶✶✶✶✶✶✶✶✶✶✶✶✶✶✶✶✶✶✶✶✶✶✶✶✶✶✶✶✶✶✶✶

hurt [hɝt] ***v.*** 使受傷
reason [ˋrizn] ***n.*** 原因

✶✶✶✶✶✶✶✶✶✶✶✶✶✶✶✶✶✶✶✶✶✶✶✶✶✶✶✶✶✶✶✶✶✶

"You are not at all like my rose. You are nowhere like her," he said to the roses. "No one has tamed you, and you have never tamed anyone. My fox was once like you. He was once a fox just like thousands of others, but I made him my friend, and now there is no one like him in all the world."

The roses were not pleased.

"You are beautiful, but you are empty," the little prince told them. "No one would die for you. Of course, an ordinary person might think that my rose looks like you, but I know that she is more important than all of you because she is the one I cared for. Because she is the one I put under a globe. Because she is the one I protected from the cold. Because she is the one I killed the caterpillars for (except for two or three that will become butterflies). Because she is the one who talked with me and who was silent with me. Because she is my rose."

Then he returned to the fox.

"Goodbye," the little prince said.

"Goodbye," said the fox. "Here is my secret. It is

very simple: We do not see clearly, except when we see it with our hearts. The most important thing cannot be easily seen with our eyes."

"The most important thing cannot be easily seen with our eyes," repeated the little prince. He wanted to be sure that he remembered this.

"The most important thing is the time you spent with your rose. That is what has made her so important."

"The most important thing is the time I spent with my rose..." repeated the little prince. He wanted to remember this.

"People have forgotten this truth," the fox told him. "But you must not forget it. You are forever responsible for what you have tamed. You are responsible for your rose..."

"I am responsible for my rose..." repeated the little prince. He wanted to remember.

* *

truth [truθ] ***n.*** 事實
responsible [rɪˋspɑnsəb!] ***adj.*** 承擔責任的

* *

chapter 22

"Good morning," said the little prince.

"Good morning," said the train signalman.

"What are you doing here?" asked the little prince.

"I move travelers around, I move thousands of travelers at one time," said the signalman. "I move the trains that they travel in. Some trains go to the right. Others go to the left."

And then a brightly-lit train hurried by. It made a noise like thunder. It shook the signalman's box.

"Those people are in a hurry," said the little prince. "What are they looking for?"

signalman [ˋsɪgn!ˏmæn] ***n.*** 信號手
move [muv] ***v.*** 搬動
thunder [ˋθʌndɚ] ***n.*** 雷聲

"Even the man who drives the train does not know that," said the signalman.

Then, a second train hurried by. It was traveling in the opposite direction.

"Are they coming back already?" asked the little prince.

"Those are not the same people," said the signalman. "That was an exchange."

"Those people were not happy where they were?"

"People are never happy in the place where they are," answered the signalman.

A third train hurried by.

"Are they trying to catch up with the first one?" asked the little prince.

* *

opposite [ˋɑpəzɪt] ***adj.*** 相反的
direction [dəˋrɛkʃən] ***n.*** 方向
exchange [ɪksˋtʃendʒ] ***v.*** 調換

* *

"They are not trying to do anything," said the signalman. "They just sleep in the train, or they yawn. Only the children press their faces up against the windows."

"The children are the only ones who know what they are looking for," said the little prince. "They spend time taking care of a doll, and the doll becomes important to them. Then if someone takes it away, they cry…"

"They are lucky," said the signalman.

chapter 23

"Good morning," said the little prince.

"Good morning," said the salesman.

The salesman sold special pills. The pills stopped people from feeling thirsty. If you took one pill every

sold [səʊld] *v.* 賣（**sell** 的過去式）
pill [pɪl] *n.* 藥

week, you would never need a drink of water.

"Why do you sell those pills?" asked the little prince.

"They save lots of time," said the salesman. "Scientists counted. These pills save fifty-three minutes every week."

"What would people do with these fifty-three minutes?"

"They do whatever they want..."

The little prince said to himself: "If I have those fifty-three minutes, I will walk slowly toward a well of fresh water."

save [sev] *v.* 節省
toward [tə`wɔrd] *prep.* 朝

Chapter 24

Eight days had passed since my plane crashed. As I listened to the little prince's story about the salesman, I drank my last drop of water.

"Ah!" I said to the little prince. "Your memories are very interesting, but I have not fixed my plane and I have no more water to drink. I would be very glad if I could walk slowly toward a well of fresh water!"

"My friend, the fox told me..."

"But my dear little friend, this has nothing to do with a fox!"

"Why?"

"Because we are going to die of thirst..."

He did not understand. He said, "It is good to have a

friend, even if one is going to die. I am very happy to have a fox as my friend…"

"He does not understand the danger," I said to myself. "He never gets hungry or thirsty. All he needs is a little sunlight…"

But then he looked at me and finally read my thoughts.

"I am thirsty, too… Let's go and search for a well of fresh water…"

I felt tired. It was silly to search for a well in a giant desert. We did not know where to search, yet we started to walk.

For hours we walked without talking. The night arrived, and the stars appeared. They looked like a dream to me, since I was feeling rather sick from being thirsty. The words from the little prince danced in front of me.

search [sɝtʃ] *v.* 在……中搜尋

"So you are thirsty, too?" I asked him.

But he did not answer me. He simply said:

"Water is good for the heart, too…"

I did not understand. Still, I did not ask what he meant… I knew that there was no need to continue asking.

He was tired and sat down. I sat next to him. After a while, he said:

"The stars are beautiful. They are beautiful because somewhere there is a flower that I cannot see from here…"

"Yes," I said, and looked at the sand under the moonlight.

"The desert is beautiful," the little prince added.

---

meant [ment] *v.* 表示……的意思（**mean** 的過去式）

And he was right. I have always loved the desert. In the desert, you sit on the sand. You see nothing. You hear nothing. Yet something beautiful fills the silence…

"The desert is beautiful," the little prince said, "because a well is hidden somewhere in it."

Suddenly I understood why the desert was beautiful. When I was a little boy, I lived in a very old house. People had always believed that the treasure was hidden inside the house. Of course, no one had ever found it. Perhaps no one had really looked for it.

But the story of the treasure created an air of mystery around the house. My house had a secret hidden deep inside it…

"Yes," I said to the little prince. "It does not matter whether we are talking about houses, stars, or the desert. What makes them beautiful cannot be seen with the eyes!"

* *

hidden [ˋhɪdn] ***adj.*** 隱藏的
treasure [ˋtrɛʒɚ] ***n.*** 金銀財寶

* *

"I am glad that you agree with my friend, the fox," he said.

Then the little prince fell asleep. I carried him in my arms as I walked.

I was touched. I felt that I was carrying a fragile treasure. I felt that there was nothing more fragile on all of Earth. In the moonlight, I looked at his pale face, his closed eyes, and his hair gently waving in the wind. I said to myself: "What I see now is only a shell. The most important part is hidden to the eyes…"

Looking at his lips open a little with a half-smile as he slept, I said to myself: "The little prince's true love for his flower touches my heart. His love shines from inside of him, like the light of a lamp. It shines even when he is asleep…" And then he seemed even more fragile to me. That light must be protected: even a little bit of wind can put it out…

Early that morning, I found the well.

* *

shine [ʃaɪn] ***v.*** 閃耀
fragile [ˋfrædʒəl] ***adj.*** 虛弱的

* *

"People hurry to get on trains," the little prince said. "But they do not know what they are looking for. So they become angry. Then they run around in circles…"

He added:

"There is no reason to do that…"

The well we had found did not look like the others in the Sahara. The wells of the Sahara are just holes dug in the sand. This one looked like a well for a village, but there was no village here. I thought that I was dreaming.

"It is strange," I said to the little prince. "Everything is ready: the pulley, the bucket, and the rope…"

* *

village [ˋvɪlɪdʒ] ***n.*** 村莊
pulley [ˋpʊlɪ] ***n.*** 滑輪
bucket [ˋbʌkɪt] ***n.*** 水桶

* *

He laughed and picked up the rope. He started to make the pulley work. It made a groaning sound like an old weather vane which the wind has long since forgotten.

"Do you hear that?" said the little prince. "We have awakened the well. Now it is singing…"

I did not want him to do all the work all by himself.

"Let me do it," I told him. "It is too heavy for you."

I slowly pulled up the bucket. I put it on the edge of the well. I could still hear the pulley singing in my ears and I saw the sunlight shining on the water.

"I am thirsty for this water," the little prince said. "Give me some to drink…"

And then I understood what he had been looking for!

I raised the bucket to his lips. He closed his eyes and drank. The water was sweet. It was as sweet as some special festival treat. This water was more than a drink. It came from our walk under the stars, the song

of the pulley, and the effort of my arms. This water was good for the heart. It was like a gift. It reminded me of Christmas when I was a little boy. The lights of the Christmas tree, the music of the Midnight Mass, and the tenderness of smiling faces were all shining because of the present I received.

The little prince said, "People on this planet grow five thousand roses in a single garden… and they still cannot find what they are looking for."

"They do not find it," I agreed.

"And yet, what they are looking for can be found in a single rose or in a drink of water…"

"Of course," I said.

"But our eyes cannot see thoroughly. We must look for it with our hearts."

I had drunk some water. I felt better. In the morning sun, the desert sand is the color of honey. I was glad to look at it. But why did I still feel sad?

"You must keep your promise," the little prince said gently. He was sitting next to me.

"What promise?"

"You know… a muzzle for my sheep… I am responsible for my flower."

I took my drawings out of my pocket. The little prince saw them and started to laugh:

"Your baobabs look like cabbages."

"Oh!" I had been so proud of my baobabs!

"And your fox… his ears… they look a little bit like horns… and they are too long!"

He laughed again. I told him:

"It is not fair, my little friend. I can only draw boa constrictors from the inside and the outside."

* *

promise [`prɑmɪs] ***n.*** 承諾
muzzle [`mʌz!] ***n.***（狗，狐等）口鼻部分

* *

"Oh! That is fine," he said. "Children will understand."

I drew a muzzle for his sheep. And I felt heartbroken when I gave it to him.

I told him: "You have plans that you have not shared with me…"

But he did not answer. Instead, he said:

"Tomorrow, you know, it will be one year since I came to the Earth…"

Then, after a moment, he said:

"Where I fell is very close to here…" he blushed.

And again, without understanding why, I felt sad. I asked him this question: "Then, the morning when I first you, you were not walking by chance in the desert? You were returning to the place where you fell?"

The little prince then blushed again. I added:

"Perhaps the reason you returned is because it has been one year since you fell on the Earth?"

He never answered my questions, but when someone blushes, that means 'Yes,' doesn't it?

"Oh!" I said. "I am afraid that you..."

But he told me:

"You should go now. Go back and work on your plane. I will wait for you here. Come back tomorrow night..."

I did not feel better. I remembered the fox. We run the risk of sorrow if we let ourselves be tamed...

chapter 26

An old stone wall stood next to the well. As I returned the next night, I could see my little prince sitting on the wall. And I heard him say:

"You do not remember? This is not the right place!"

Someone must have answered him because he then said:

"Oh, yes, yes! Today is definitely the day, but this is not the place..."

I kept walking toward the wall. I did not see or hear anyone except the little prince. However, he spoke again:

"... Of course. You will see my footprints in the

✶✶✶✶✶✶✶✶✶✶✶✶✶✶✶✶✶✶✶✶✶✶✶✶✶✶✶✶✶✶✶✶✶

wall [wɔl] ***n.*** 牆，壁；圍牆；城牆

✶✶✶✶✶✶✶✶✶✶✶✶✶✶✶✶✶✶✶✶✶✶✶✶✶✶✶✶✶✶✶✶✶

sand. All you have to do is wait for me. I will be there tonight."

I was twenty feet away from the wall. I still saw nothing.

After a moment, the little prince asked:

"You have good poison? You are sure that it will not make me suffer too long?"

I stopped. My heart was beating hard, but I still did not understand.

"Now go away," he said. "I want to get down of this wall."

Then I looked at the bottom of the wall. I was in shock! There before me, facing the little prince was one of those yellow snakes that can kill you in thirty seconds. I reached for my gun and took a step back. The snake must have heard me since it slipped through the sand and disappeared among the stones.

* *

poison [ˋpɔɪzn] ***n.*** 毒藥

* *

I got to the wall and caught the little prince in my arms. His face was as white as snow.

"What is going on here? Why are you talking to a snake?"

I untied his scarf. I wiped his forehead. I made him drink some water. But I was afraid to ask him any questions. He looked at me gravely. Then he put his arms around my neck. I could feel his heart beating. It sounded like the heart of a dying bird that had been shot.

* *

forehead [ˋfɔr͵hɛd] ***n.*** 前額

* *

He said:

"I am glad that you had fixed your plane. Now you can go home..."

"How did you know that?" I cried. I was just about to tell him that I had finally fixed my plane!

He did not answer me, but he said:

"Today I am going home, too…"

He went on, sadly, "It is much farther away... it will be much more difficult..."

Something strange and terrible was happening. I held the little prince in my arms as if he was a baby, yet no matter what I did, I felt that he was somehow slipping away from me.

His eyes were full of sadness. He looked like he was lost, far away.

✶✶✶✶✶✶✶✶✶✶✶✶✶✶✶✶✶✶✶✶✶✶✶✶✶✶✶✶✶✶✶✶

fix [fɪkst] ***v.*** 修理

✶✶✶✶✶✶✶✶✶✶✶✶✶✶✶✶✶✶✶✶✶✶✶✶✶✶✶✶✶✶✶✶

I said, "I have your sheep. And I have the box for your sheep. And the muzzle..."

He smiled sadly.

I waited for a long time. I thought that he might be feeling better. I said:

"My little friend, you are afraid... "

He was afraid, of course! But he laughed lightly and said, "I will be much more afraid tonight..."

Once again, I was frozen with fear and I realized how terrible I would feel if I never heard his laugh again. For me, that laugh was like a well of fresh water in the desert.

"My little friend, I want to hear you laugh again..."

But he said to me:

"Tonight, it will be one year since I arrived here. My

* *

afraid [ə`fred] ***adj.*** 害怕的

* *

star can be found just above the place where I fell one year ago…"

"My little friend, please tell me that the matter of the snake and the star is nothing but a bad dream."

But he did not answer my question. He said to me:

"The things that are most important cannot be seen…"

"Of course…"

"It is like my flower. If you love a flower that lives on a star, it makes you happy to look at the night sky. All the stars look like flowers…"

"Of course…"

"It is like the water. The water you gave me to drink was like music. The pulley and the rope were singing… You remember… how beautiful it was…"

"Of course…"

"You will look up at the stars at night. My star, my home, is too small for me to show you. It will be better like that. My little star will simply be one of the stars for you so you will love to look at the stars. They will all be your friends. I will also give you a gift..." He laughed again.

"Ah! My little friend, my little friend, how much I love to hear you laugh!"

"That will be my gift… it will be like the water."

"What do you mean?"

"To different people, the stars mean different things. For travelers, the stars guide them. For others, they are nothing but small lights in the sky. For people who are scholars, the stars are problems to think about. For businessman, they are made of gold. But all these stars are silent. You will have stars like no one else.

"What do you mean?"

scholar [ˋskɑlɚ] ***n.*** 學者
silent [ˋsaɪlənt] ***adj.*** 不作聲的

"You will look at the sky at night... and since I live on one of the stars and since I will be laughing on that star, you will hear all the stars laughing. Only you will have stars that can laugh!"

And he laughed again.

"And when you don't feel sad anymore (time heals sadness), you will be glad that you have known me. You will always be my friend. You will want to laugh with me, and sometimes, you will open your window... and your friends will be surprised to see you laughing as you look up at the sky. You will tell them: 'Yes, looking at the stars always makes me laugh!' They will think that you are crazy. It will be a trick that I shall have played on you."

And he laughed again.

"It is as if I gave you little bells instead of stars and they know how to laugh..." He laughed again. Then he looked serious. He said, "Tonight… you know… do not come back."

✶✶✶✶✶✶✶✶✶✶✶✶✶✶✶✶✶✶✶✶✶✶✶✶✶✶✶✶✶✶✶✶✶

trick [trɪk] ***n.*** 把戲

✶✶✶✶✶✶✶✶✶✶✶✶✶✶✶✶✶✶✶✶✶✶✶✶✶✶✶✶✶✶✶✶✶

I said to him, "I will not leave you."

"It should look like I am hurting... It should look almost like I am dying. It will look like that. Do not come to see that. There is no need."

"I will not leave you."

But he was worried.

"I tell you this," he said, "Because I don't want the snake to bite you. Snakes are terrible. Snakes may bite you just for fun…"

"I will not leave you."

But then another thought made him feel better: "It is true that they have no more poison for a second bite."

That night I did not see him leave. He disappeared without a sound.

* *

dying [ˋdaɪɪŋ] *adj.* 垂死的
bite [baɪt] *v.* 咬

* *

When I finally found him, he was walking quickly. He only said:

"Oh! You are here…"

And he took my hand. But he was still worried:

"It was wrong for you to come. You will be sad. It should look like I am dying, and that will not be true…"

I said nothing.

"You understand. My home is very far. I cannot bring this body with me. It is too heavy."

I said nothing.

"But this body will be like an empty shell, like the bark of an old tree. That is not sad…"

I said nothing.

He was sad, but he tried to be cheerful:

"It will be wonderful, you know. Just like you, I will be looking at the stars. All the stars will be like wells of fresh water with rusty pulleys and I will drink water from the stars..."

I said nothing.

"It will be so beautiful! You will have five-hundred million bells, and I will have five-hundred million wells…"

Then he was quiet. He was crying…

"This is the place. Let me walk ahead by myself."

He sat down because he was afraid. He said again:

"You know... My flower... I am responsible for her! And she is so fragile! She knows so little. She has only four small thorns to protect herself against all the world..."

I sat down as well because I could no longer stand.

He said:

"You know... That is all..."

The little prince stopped for only a moment. Then he stood up. He moved a step. I could not move.

There was nothing but a flash of yellow close to his ankle. For a moment, he stood very still. He did not cry out. He fell as gently as a tree. He did not even make a sound because of the sand..

fell [fɛl] *v.* 倒下（**fall** 過去式）

chapter 27

Now, of course, six years have already gone by… I have never told this story before. My friends were very glad to find out that I was alive. I was sad, but I told them: "I am just tired…"

These days I feel much better, but not entirely. I know that the little prince has returned to his planet. I know this because when I went back the next morning, I did not find his body. And his body was not very big… And now, at night, I love to listen to the stars. They sound like five-hundred million bells…

But there is something strange. I drew the muzzle for the little prince, but I forgot to draw the strap for it! He will not be able to put it on his sheep. So I asked myself:

* *

entirely [ɪnˋtaɪrlɪ] ***adv.*** 完全地
strap [stræp] ***n.*** 帶子

* *

"What has happened on his planet? Perhaps the sheep has eaten the flower…"

Sometimes I say to myself: "Of course not! The little prince puts his flower under a glass globe each night. He takes care of his sheep carefully…" Then I feel better. And I hear all the stars laughing sweetly.

At some other times I tell myself, "Everyone sometimes doesn't pay attention. But one time would be enough! Perhaps one night he forgot the glass globe for his flower, or perhaps the sheep got out of his box one night…"

Then all my bells turn into tears!

It is a great mystery. For those who love the little prince, nothing in the universe can be the same if somewhere, somehow a sheep we have never seen has or has not eaten a certain flower…

✶✶✶✶✶✶✶✶✶✶✶✶✶✶✶✶✶✶✶✶✶✶✶✶✶✶✶✶✶✶✶✶✶

carefully [ˋkɛrfəlɪ] ***adv.*** 小心謹慎地
Perhaps [pɚˋhæps] ***adv.*** 可能
somehow [ˋsʌmˏhaʊ] ***adv.*** 由於某種未知的原因；不知怎麼的
certain [ˋsɝtən] ***adj.*** 某（一位……人）

✶✶✶✶✶✶✶✶✶✶✶✶✶✶✶✶✶✶✶✶✶✶✶✶✶✶✶✶✶✶✶✶✶

Look up at the sky. Ask yourself: "He has the sheep eaten or not eaten the flower?" And you will see how everything changes…

And no one grown-up will ever understand why this is important!

For me, this is the loveliest and saddest place in the world. It is the same place I drew on the previous page. I drew it again to make sure you understand it. This is the place where the little prince first arrived on the Earth and where he left.

Look at it carefully so that you will recognize this place if you travel some day in the African desert. If you find yourself in this place, do not hurry. Stop there for a moment right under the star!

And then, if a child comes to you, and laughs, and has golden hair, and does not answer you questions, you

✶✶✶✶✶✶✶✶✶✶✶✶✶✶✶✶✶✶✶✶✶✶✶✶✶✶✶✶✶✶

same [sem] ***adj.***（通常與 **the** 連用）同一的
previous [ˋpriviəs] ***adj.*** 先前的
drawn [drɔn] ***adj.*** 畫（**draw** 的過去分詞）
recognize [ˋrɛkəgˏnaɪz] ***v.*** 認出

✶✶✶✶✶✶✶✶✶✶✶✶✶✶✶✶✶✶✶✶✶✶✶✶✶✶✶✶✶✶

will know who he is. If this happens, save me from my sadness! Write to me immediately that he has come back...

THE END

★★★★★★★★★★★★★★★★★★★★★★★★★★★★★★★★

write to [raɪt tu] 寫信給……

★★★★★★★★★★★★★★★★★★★★★★★★★★★★★★★★